Jesse Jameson

and the Bogie Beast

Sean Wright

25-10-03

542 OF 2500

A Crowswing Book

LET THE JOURNEY BEGIN ...

Jesse Jameson Series

Otherwise known as the Jesse Jameson **Alpha to Omega** Series
(Reading order)

This is the second book in the
Jesse Jameson Alpha to Omega Series written
by Sean Wright and the author dedicates it to his
mother, June, and his father, John,
who made it all possible.

First published in hardback in 2003 by Crowswing Books.

10 9 8 7 6 5 4 3 2 1

www.crowswingbooks.co.uk

(Special Limited Edition 2500)

A CIP catalogue record for this book is available from the British Library.

ISBN 0-9544374-6-2

CONTENTS

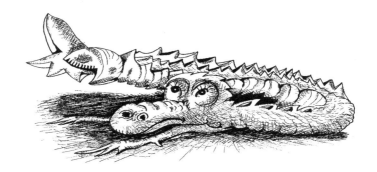

To transform is a noble and dying art, but to transcend is the birthright of every living creature in the human and fairy kingdoms ...

Praise for Sean Wright

'Highly recommended to all fans of children's literature...' *www.sqwubbsybooks.co.uk*

'Congratulations on the success of your books!' *www.fantasticfiction.co.uk*

'Wright's books are full of adventure and magic.' *Eastern Daily Press*

'I have read and enjoyed Jesse Jameson and the Golden Glow and can see why you have so many fans...' *Caradoc King, Philip Pullman's Literary Agent*

'Brilliant!' *Kidswise* Magazine

'Has the reader hooked from the first page till the last.' *The Teacher* Magazine

'Readers and listeners alike were spellbound by Jesse's adventures with witches and warlocks ....' *BBC Radio Cambridgeshire (Big Rea-a-thon 2003)*

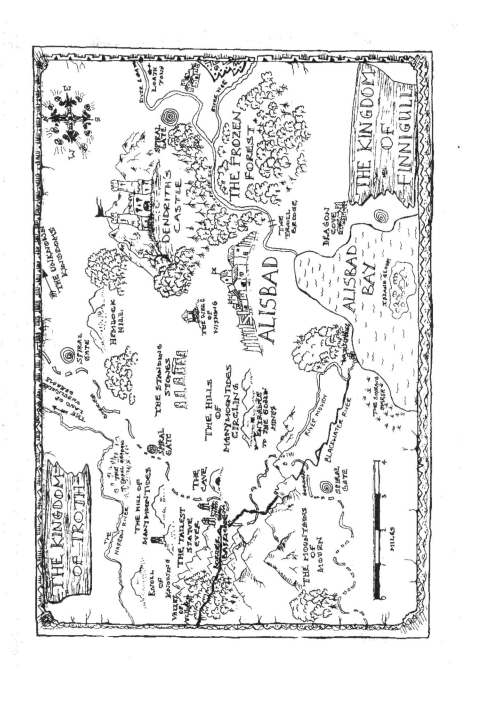

One

Home Sweet Home

From the moment Jesse Jameson was led up the garden path towards her house, a bad feeling butterflied inside her stomach. She clutched her mother's hand as hard as she could, in anticipation of the screaming Scratchits.

'Don't worry, Jesse,' Cathal Jameson said. 'The Scratchits will be out before you know it.'

'But what if they refuse?'

'Then Franklin Lampard, my solicitor, will begin legal proceedings to have them evicted.'

'What if there's a dreadful argument when we knock on the door?'

'Knock? On my own door? That'll be the day! I'll walk straight in!' Cathal Jameson roared. 'And as for arguing, I can give as good as I get.'

'What if Dad doesn't want us? What if he wants them instead? What if-'

'Jesse,' Cathal cut in. She looked lovingly into her daughter's sparkling blue eyes. The look she got back reminded her so much of Roger, her husband. 'Dad'll want us. As soon as the glamour has worn off, he'll be back to his old self in no time at all. So don't you go worrying yourself. Everything is going to turn out fine. Do you hear?'

'Yes, Mum.'

But Jesse wasn't convinced. For one thing, the house was different. It had been painted, a yucky mustard colour. Only three days ago it had been white. The small rose bush below Jesse's bedroom window had doubled in size. The weeping cherry tree in the middle of the lawn had grown at least a metre. And the laurel hedge was out of control!

'Something's wrong,' Jesse whispered. 'Something is terribly wrong. The garden has gone mad.'

'Fairy Time is a funny thing, Jesse.'

'How do you mean?'

'I suppose I've got used to it over the years. An odd half an hour in the Kingdom of Troth here and there was fine at weekends when I was child. But-'

'You used to go to Troth when you were a child?' Jesse said incredulously. 'Amazing.'

'My human parents, your Grandma and Granddad Longley, were glamoured so they never ever knew.'

'You mean they were hypnotised?'

'Kind of. During the summer holidays, the year before I left school, I spent the entire six weeks holiday there. It was great to take the new Time Stoppers.'

'What's a Time Stopper?'

'It's a magic potion that was created by the more forward-thinking Elders to level out time in the Fairy Kingdoms and the human world. If you took a Time Stopper, then the same amount of time passed in all the kingdoms, including the human one.

'You see, before the Time Stopper potion, one day in Fairy Time equalled a year and a day in human time. It still does, unless you take the potion.'

'But I wasn't given any Time Stopper potion when I arrived in Troth,' Jesse said.

Cathal's face coloured red with anger. 'Perigold! That old fool! He's always been fanatical about old values and traditions. He hates any kind of change. I had a massive argument with him when I was your age and he discovered I was taking Time Stoppers. He brought out all the old arguments to try and put me off. Things like it *being unnatural*, and *messing with the will of the gods*, and yes ...

perhaps the most convincing one of all: *the dangers of possible side effects*. But taking the potion is the only way to stop the ageing process.'

'How do you mean?'

'As I said earlier, one day in Fairy Time equals a year and a day in human time. You've been away about ... three days in human time?'

'Yes.'

'So...' Jesse tried to work out the calculations mentally, but her mind was spinning; not at the difficulty of the calculation but at what she knew to be the horrifying truth.

'You've been away three years and three days, Jesse.'

'Three years and three days!' Jesse gulped. 'That's awful! I'm almost fourteen? Look at me? I'm an eleven year old stuck in a fourteen year old body!'

'It's not that bad,' Cathal tried to reassure her, trying to hide her anger at Perigold.

'Bad? It's ... it's absolutely disastrous! I'm ancient!'

Cathal laughed, which made Jesse feel very annoyed. Her mother just didn't understand. She had missed three years of her life!

'All my friends will be grown up!'

'A little older, yes. But not grown up.'

'Oh, Mum, this is terrible,' Jesse said, shaking her head sadly. 'My life is ruined.'

'Try to think of the positive things.'

'Positive things?' Jesse waved her hands about wildly. 'What positive things?'

'Well ...'

'You see. You can't think of any, can you? This is really bad. Briggsie will be shaving by now. He'll be as hairy as a bear. How disgusting!'

'He'll also be at High School, but let's not get too down-hearted, Jesse. We must-'

'Oh, Mum, it just gets worse. High School? GCSEs! I'm still struggling with my times tables up to the tens! I don't understand half the things Mrs Wobble talks about. Pronouns, and prepo-whatsits, and gravity and all that science stuff. I'll never pass GCSE exams. I've lost three years of learning. This is so awful.'

'Now listen,' Cathal said, adopting adult tones. 'Let's not get carried away. If you think about it logically, it's not that bad. For one thing, you'll be out of Wormdirt's Primary. You never did like Mrs Wobble, now did you?'

Jesse shook her head in agreement. Wormdirt's lived up to its name and reputation. It had been a horrible experience from reception right the way through to Mrs Wobble's class.

'And another thing: we can hire a private tutor so that you can catch up.'

'It sounds horrible. I'll have to spend all my free time studying. My life is ruined.'

'We'll discuss this later,' Cathal said,

producing a key from her pocket. She was a tall, slender woman, with shoulder-length blonde hair, and kind blue eyes. She was wearing a long black coat, jeans, and brown ankle boots.

The key slid easily into the lock.

Click.

Cathal pushed open the door and Jesse followed her into the hallway. They stood there for a long time, mouths wide, gawking at the sight before them. Everything had changed - the colour of the walls, the carpet, the curtains. And there was more.

'What's happened to all my furniture?' Cathal said at last, unable to hide her bewilderment.

'I don't know,' Jesse said shakily. 'Are you sure we're in the right house?'

Cathal nodded and walked across the hallway to the closed door of the living room. Slowly, she turned the handle, and inched it open.

Jesse peered into the room, and shook her head in disbelief. There was nothing in here that she recognised. This couldn't be their house, could it? Then there was the smell of the house. It smelled old and damp, not at all like it used to smell - freshly baked bread, aromatic coffee, and jasmine-scented pot pourri.

'Roger? We're home! Where are you?' Cathal called.

Jesse jumped, swung around to see that her mother had moved into the hallway and was now striding purposefully towards the kitchen door.

'Be careful, Mum,' Jesse said. 'Don't do anything foolish. Please.'

'Don't worry, Jesse,' Cathal said in a calm voice. 'I'm big enough to take care of us both.'

Jesse hurried into the hallway, and clutched her mother's outstretched hand. Briefly, she glanced at the staircase which led to her bedroom. A terrible thought struck her: Bonnie! She had to find her pet hamster, Bonnie!

Then another thought swiftly followed: Roamer? Where was their black Labrador? He usually greeted them at the door, barking excitedly, his tail wagging wildly.

'I'm scared, Mum,' Jesse said. 'Something awful has happened. Where is Roamer?'

'I was wondering the same thing,' Cathal said. 'Maybe he's out in the garden.'

Jesse saw the look of doubt in her mother's eyes. She was as worried as Jesse, but wasn't admitting it.

'Can we go upstairs first?' Jesse asked. 'I want to see if Bonnie is all right.'

'Listen, love,' Cathal said softly. 'I ... er ... don't know how to put this, but don't go building up your hopes concerning Bonnie. All right?'

'What do you mean?'

'There's no easy way to say this. Hamsters have short life spans. Two to three years max.'

Jesse suddenly felt dizzy and little sick.

'You think she's ... dead, don't you?'

'There's a good chance, Jesse.'

Jesse let go of her mother's hand and raced as fast as she could up the stairs, crashing through her bedroom door. Only this room wasn't a bedroom anymore. It looked like a junk room, with all kinds of things - from old kettles and TVs to shelves filled with smelly antique books. Where her bed used to be she saw a pile of crates, containing magazines and ornaments and bric-a-brac. There was no sign of anything she recognised. And no sign of Bonnie.

'Come on, love,' Cathal said, standing in the doorway, with her arms open wide. 'Let's check the kitchen.'

A minute later they opened the kitchen door. Jesse's face dropped with horror. Two old people sat at a table, sipping tea. They both smiled almost simultaneously.

'Pot's brewed,' the old woman said, nodding towards the tea cosy in the middle of the table. 'Now yours is a weak one without sugar, isn't it, love?'

Cathal looked at Jesse, then at the woman, and then back at Jesse again. Her face was a cloud of confusion.

'And you, young lady,' the old man said to

Jesse, 'will be expecting a ... now let me see ... ah, yes, a lemonade.'

Cathal said what Jesse was thinking.

'Do we know you?'

'I know that this might seem odd, Mrs Jameson,' the old man said. He was in his eighties, with a bald head and wrinkly face that reminded Jesse of a dried prune. 'But we've a great deal of experience house-sitting, haven't we, Maude?'

'Oh, yes, a great deal of experience,' the old woman nodded, slurping more tea.

'Not that we get paid much, because we don't, do we, Maude?'

'Pennies. We only just make ends meet. But we're too old now to change our ways. Jobs are hard to find when you get to our age, aren't they, Claude?'

'You can say that again, Maude.'

'I said jobs are hard to come by when your-'

'I heard you the first time. Have you turned down your hearing aid thingy again?'

'Must have turned down my hearing aid thing,' Maude said, fiddling behind her ear. 'Ah, that's better. Now what were you saying?'

'Never mind that now, dear. We've got guests.'

Claude motioned with his bony old hand at Jesse and her mother.

'Pull up a chair, you two. You look

exhausted.'

'Yes, have a drink.' Maude pointed at a large uncut sponge cake next to the teapot. 'Help yourself. It's freshly made.'

Neither Jesse nor Cathal accepted the woman's offer.

'Now then, tell us all about the Fairy Kingdoms,' Claude said after he had given them drinks. 'We're desperate to hear all the gossip, aren't we?'

'Desperate,' Maude said. 'We miss Troth so much while we look after other people's homes, don't we, dear?'

'Are some folk still taking those wretched Time Stopper potions? Doing us out of a job, they are. Awful stuff.'

Jesse was in a state of stunned silence. What were they talking about? Who were these people? Did Mum know them? Long lost relatives, maybe? House-sitting? All the gossip? Troth? Time Stoppers? Jesse's mind was drowning in questions.

At last Cathal managed to compose herself enough to speak.

'Who are you and what are you doing in our home?'

'Ah, yes, I can see you're a little upset and confused,' Claude said.

'Only natural,' Maude added.

'Poor dears.'

'What a shock for you both.'

'It can't be easy, coming home to a house full of strangeness and strangers, now can it, Maude?'

'Never easy, dear. Still - we must get down to the what's what and who's whos, mustn't we?'

'Yes, quite.' Claude cleared his throat. 'Sorry to give you such a surprise. Here you are.'

Cathal took the letter which Claude slid across the table and read:

Dear Cathal and Jesse,

Where to begin? At the beginning I suppose.

I've just found out from a very good friend of mine, who had business in the human kingdom, that the Scratchits charmed Roger Jameson into selling the house. That was two and half years ago in human time.

The Scratchits and Roger then left for the Kingdom of Finnigull, after spending all the money from the sale of the house on a luxury trip around the world.

When the new owners put the house up for sale, I bought it back again - a year ago in human time.

The deeds to the house are in your name Cathal, and they are in the safe hands of your solicitor, Mr

Lampard senior, of Lampard, Lampard, and Shoeshine. I employed Claude and Maude to house-sit for you while you were gone. The house will be empty the moment they leave, and all of your old furniture will be returned as good as new.

Yours truly

A friend

Jesse and Cathal re-read the letter, hardly believing their eyes.

'So, there you have it,' Claude said. 'We will, of course, leave your house the way it used to be, won't we, Maude?'

'I suppose so,' Maude said, sighing. 'I really am getting very tired of all this moving from one house to another. Where are we next?'

Slowly, and very shakily, Claude took out a pair of half-moon glasses and propped them on the tip of his bulbous red nose. He then produced a letter from his pocket written on yellowing parchment and read it.

'House-sitting location ... blah, blah, blah ... Washington DC ... blahdy, blahdy, blah ... the Bushtons, Hilary and George ... retired shape-shifters ... blah, blah, blah ... take the first left on Capital Hill ... expected return ... three years and three days in human time. Be prompt, this time. No catching up on gossip.'

'I hate it when they say that - *no catching up on gossip*. They have no idea how frustrating it is not to know the latest stories, do they, Claude?'

'Clueless, my dear.' Claude narrowed his eyes, and winked. 'I bet you two have a fair few tales to tell, being recently returned from the Fairy Kingdoms? Eh?'

'A few,' Cathal said cautiously.

Jesse's head suddenly ignited with all of her past adventures in the Kingdoms of Troth and Finnigull. She thought about the fantastical discovery of being a changeling, a fairy child exchanged at birth with a human baby. Then there were the great friendships she had struck with the soothsayer, Perigold, the Dragon Hunter, Richard, and the magical Gobitt, Iggywig. Returning to the Fairy Kingdoms to embark on three dangerous quests was a thrilling time in her life. When she helped to defeat the evil witch, Dendrith, thus ensuring the rescue of Cathal Jameson, Jesse's dealings with the Fairy Kingdoms seemed complete.

But now the house-sitters loomed large in her life. Would she ever be free from the magical powers of other worlds?

'Who wrote the letter?' Cathal wanted to know.

'Can't say,' Maude said nonchalantly. 'We

are not privy to such information, are we, Claude?'

'No, dear. We go where the Shape-Shifters' Care and Benevolent Trust send us. It's a thankless job, but some old shapoes have got to do it, I suppose. It just happens to be us.'

'You are shape-shifters?' Jesse asked.

'Used to be,' Claude said, raising his eyebrows.

'What happened to your powers?'

'We're not allowed to discuss it, are we, Maude?'

Maude shuffled uncomfortably in her chair. There was an awkward silence. Jesse thought that Maude's cheeks had turned a brighter shade of pink. She was clearly embarrassed.

'So, if you've finished your drinks,' Maude said to Jesse and her mother at last. 'It's best if you wait outside until we've finished packing. We won't be long. And it's less dangerous for you if you've cleared the premises completely. Isn't that right, Claude?'

'Yes, Maude. I couldn't have put it better myself.'

With this, they both stood up and joined hands.

'Stand clear, please,' Maude said, nodding for Jesse and Cathal to go outside through the patio doors. 'Here we go again.'

Jesse and her mother walked outside, and

turned to watch in amazement. Claude and Maude turned purple, then green, and then an electric shade of blue. They pulled the most incredible faces at each other - pouting lips, blowing out cheeks, gnashing false teeth, blowing out cheeks, crossing-eyes, blowing out cheeks, waggling tongues, blowing out cheeks, wiggling ears, blowing out cheeks, thumbing noses, blowing out cheeks. Finally, thick red smoke rose up from their slippers and filled the kitchen, completely blocking them from sight.

Jesse looked at her bedroom window and saw more red smoke filling the room. It poured out of the chimney and formed great red clouds in the sky. Then there came a tremendous flash of yellow light, and a massive loud bang! Bang! BANG! The smoke vanished and so, too, did Claude and Maude and all of their belongings and furniture.

Two

Kildrith

'That was unreal!' Jesse cried.

Cathal nodded her agreement. They both watched in silent awe as the empty house filled from nowhere with their old familiar furniture; decorated magically from top to bottom - just the way it had been four years ago.

'I don't believe my eyes,' Jesse said, walking around the house a few moments later. 'Everything is back to the way it used to be.'

Cathal picked up a silver frame from the kitchen worktop. It showed a photograph of her, Jesse, Roger, and Roamer.

'Not quite everything,' Cathal said sadly.

'No, not quite everything,' Jesse echoed.

They sat down opposite each other at the kitchen table.

'We need to talk,' Cathal said at last.

'About what?'

'Everything that has happened recently.'

'Our family, you mean? Our crazy mixed up fairy family?'

'Yes. That's right, Jesse. Are you ready to talk about our crazy mixed up fairy family?'

Jesse shook her head. 'Perigold confused me enough in the Knoll of Knowing. I just don't get all this fairy stuff. It makes my head hurt.'

'But it's important that you understand.'

'But it's too difficult.'

'I agree, it is not easy, but-'

'If it concerns ... *him,*' she said with a loathing in her voice, 'I don't want to know.' Jesse found it hard to talk about the Bogie Beast. She had tried to block him from her mind. But she just couldn't shake the gruesome image of her visions. In truth, he scared her.

'No, it doesn't concern *him.* It concerns me and you. It concerns the very root of where we come from.'

'How do you mean?'

'Changelings are drawn to the Fairy Kingdoms at around the age of ten years. It's a time for them to be educated in fairy ways, to share the stories they have gathered and provide the Elders with valuable insights into the ever-changing behaviour and customs of humans.'

'But I wasn't drawn in, was I?'

'Not in the same way that others have been drawn, no. You came to rescue me from the Dark Kingdom of Finnigull. No other changeling child has ever done that before. There is nothing subtle about the stories you have created. You have whipped up quite a storm in the fairy worlds.'

'Have I?'

'Yes, a mighty one. News of your adventures even reached as far as Dendrith's Dungeons, while I was imprisoned there. Completing Brimbalin's trades earned you a great deal of respect. I'm sure the defeat of Dendrith and our escape from her castle will have caused a huge stir.'

'But it wasn't me. It was Perigold, the Dragon Hunter, and Iggywig who made it all possible.'

'True, but you started the Rumble. It will grow into a deafening noise of discontent now.'

'The Rumble? What is that?'

'It's partly people's thoughts and actions, and it's partly a living force - a creature of sorts that feeds on discontent. Rescuing me has begun its passage throughout all the Fairy Kingdoms.

'You see, all changeling children return now and again to the Fairy Kingdoms. It makes it easier for them to understand the fairy ways. As you have seen, fairies have remarkable powers which humans find hard to accept. Once upon a time, thousands of years ago, we interacted freely with humans. We helped each other. We lived together in peace. There was no Rumble, just the Calm. But all that had to change, because we were bullied, singled-out as odd and weird. We retreated back into the Fairy Kingdoms, and slammed shut the door to the human world, with the one exception of the Changeling Tradition.'

'Is that why you glamoured Grandma and Granddad Longley?'

'In a way. Don't get me wrong, your human grandparents were wonderful people. But it was best that they didn't know too much about my childhood visits to the Fairy Kingdoms.'

'Would it have been hard for them to accept?'

'Maybe. But the real reason was to protect them. You see, there are a few Dark Kingdom families who continue the Changeling Tradition. But their reasons are not noble. They change fairy children with human children because they are trying to control the human world.'

'How?'

'It's really rather simple. They put their fairy children into the homes of the rich and powerful. World famous leaders in many walks of life are at this very moment being influenced by the fairy children of the Dark Kingdoms. They have no idea that they are being manipulated.'

'It sounds unbelievable,' Jesse said.

'It is, but sadly it's true.'

They sat there in silence for awhile, each with their own thoughts. At last, Cathal spoke what was really on her mind.

'I was not happy when they took you from me - just after you were born. Even though I understood the reasons for the exchange with a human baby - to enrich our bank of precious stories and to gain insights into human behaviour - I felt cheated and robbed. You were and still are, after all, my child.'

Jesse listened carefully. She felt very sad that her Mum was close to tears. She reached out and held her hand.

'You see, there are a few fairy people, not many, who have dared to question the noble Changeling Tradition that your grandfather, Perigold, holds so dear. Even though I'm part of that tradition myself, and spent my early years just like you in the human world, I dared to break the tradition and paid the price.'

'What price?'

'I was exiled to the human world.'

'What do you mean?'

'I was no longer welcome in the Fairy Kingdoms. I came back to the human world to find you and bring you up as my own child, pretending to be human. This had never been done before. The Elders of the Kingdom of Troth were very angry. I had broken their *precious* tradition. But they didn't understand. How could they? They hadn't given birth to you. Only a mother understands how badly her heart is broken when her baby has been taken away. I had to be with you. And so it was.

'While the human child's real parents slept one dark, cold night, I returned their baby to them. It was a wonderful moment being able to return their own flesh and blood, and take you and hold you once more.'

'Oh, Mum,' Jesse said, cuddling up to Cathal.

'The first couple of years were difficult, bringing you up on my own, but somehow we muddled through. Then I met your Dad - the handsome, young Roger Jameson. We married and he accepted you completely as his own child. He was caring, understanding, and patient with you. We were very much in love. Then, that day in the woods, I was kidnapped by Dendrith, and you did the one thing that no other changeling has ever done before: you returned to rescue a fairy that had been banished from her own homeland.'

'I would do it again,' Jesse said, hugging Cathal even tighter.

'I am very proud of you, Jesse.'

They hugged for awhile, and then Jesse had a thought.

'So what are we going to do now?'

'There is only one thing we can do: we have to return and find Dad and Roamer.'

'I agree,' Jesse said, nodding. 'But where will we start?'

'If we can find the Scratchits,' Cathal reasoned, 'then we'll find Dad.'

When Jesse went to bed that evening, she found it hard to sleep. Over and over the thought of the bullying Scratchits resurfaced. Over and over she couldn't shift the image of the final battle with Dendrith. The crazy witch's evil eyes kept flashing into her mind, the Surgeons' scalpels aimed right at her heart. Over and over she thought long and hard about the strange letter they had been given by Claude and Maude. Who had bought back their house for them? Where were Dad and Roamer? What had happened to Bonnie?

Eventually, she drifted into a deep sleep but it didn't last long.

Jesse's mind whirled. She fell into a repeating vision, which she couldn't control. Countless times it came and went. It was the most hideous nightmare. She could see that she was in a dark, damp dungeon. She shivered in a corner, rubbing her arms to keep warm. Through the gloom of the one single candle which lit the dungeon, she could see a malformed shadow. It advanced slowly, wheezing with every icy breath. It reached out its long, pale fingers, opening its luminous green slits of eyes, and whispered, 'So good to see you. Soon we shall be together again ...'

Jesse woke up in bed with a jolt, and hurried into her mother's room. Cathal was already awake, looking as disturbed as Jesse.

'Come here, darling,' she said, hugging Jesse. 'It's all right.'

Jesse listened with a stunned expression on her face, as her mum described the nightmare. The visions had been identical in every detail.

'What's going on, Mum?'

'We must leave, right now. Fetch your clothes and get dressed. Hurry. He's coming.'

'The Beast, you mean?'

Cathal nodded, and bit nervously on her bottom lip.

Jesse hurried to her room, gathered her clothes, and dressed quickly in her mother's bedroom.

'But where are we going?' Jesse said.

Cathal looked suspiciously around the room. She seemed to be searching for something. Then she moved to the window, peering out from behind the closed bedroom curtains. The street lamps below illuminated sections of the gleaming wet pavement. But there were dark places, shadowy places that might have harboured hidden dangers. There was no way of knowing for certain how close the Bogie Beast or one of his minions might be.

'Who's out there?' Jesse said, moving closer to the curtain to peer out.

'Stay back,' Cathal commanded. 'I thought I saw something move behind the Briggs's fence.'

'Are you sure?'

Cathal turned and faced her daughter.

'Yes.'

'Is ... he ... here?'

'Are you ready?' Cathal said, avoiding Jesse's question.

'Er ... yes ... I think so.'

'Let's go. Hold my hand. And whatever happens, don't let go. Do you understand?'

Jesse nodded, the glow of fear in her eyes growing. Quickly, she followed her mother downstairs and out into the murk of the night.

Jesse found herself clutching the gift she had been given by the Gobitt. She wondered what the two leather bags held inside. Maybe soon she would find out.

'Keep to the shadows,' Cathal whispered. 'Stay low.'

They crossed the deserted road and paused outside the Briggs's house. Jesse wondered what

Jake Briggs looked like now that he was fourteen. His bedroom light was on, which struck Jesse as odd, because it was three o'clock in the morning.

Someone turned the corner into Chestnut Road, a tall shadowy figure, with heavy clomping footfalls. The figure began to run towards them.

'Hide,' Cathal said, dragging Jesse into Jake Briggs's garden. They dived behind a bush, crouching low, eyes as wide as a full moon, and waited.

The running footfalls slowed to a steady walk.

Jesse could hardly control her trembling hands as she took out the two bags. She gave one to her mother and motioned silently for her to loosen the drawstring.

'What's in here?' Cathal whispered.

'I don't know,' Jesse confessed. 'It's a gift from Iggywig.'

They both smiled and whispered together: 'Short-Fused Charm.'

Clearly, Jesse's mother was well aware of the capability of such wonderful magic.

The footfalls slowed as they reached the house next-door. Jesse slid one finger inside the bag, ready to yank it open and tip out the contents. A dog howled close by, a haunting wolf-like cry that made Jesse draw in a sharp, cold breath. Her heart hammered in her chest.

Her mouth was dry and sticky.

'Don't move a muscle,' Cathal whispered. 'Get ready.'

The figure stopped at the gate, twisted around, and removed its dark hood.

Jesse opened the bag. Cathal did the same.

Just then the front door was wrenched open, and Mrs Briggs stood there in her dressing gown. 'Come on in, Charlie, love,' she said to the figure. 'You'll catch your death standing out here. You've done enough for one night. Come on in. Kettle's boiled.'

'I searched the north end of the wood, by the river,' Charlie Briggs said. 'Nothing.'

'Come on, love,' Mrs Briggs urged. 'Leave it for tonight, eh?'

Charlie Briggs strode past them and into the house. The door slammed shut. There was a click as the key turned in the lock.

Jesse shifted around on her haunches, and shook her head in disbelief at the sight which now greeted her. In the living-room window of the Briggs's house was a poster of her and Jake. The poster read:

MISSING

Have you seen these children?
They were last spotted on November
10th, three years ago, heading
in the direction of Millburn Wood.

Contact Millburn Police on 7208 765480.
All information will be treated in
the strictest confidence.

'I don't believe it,' Jesse said, shaking her head. 'Jake went missing the day I stepped into the fairy ring. What has happened to him?'

'Maybe he followed you in.'

'Then where is he?'

'Who has him, you mean? Humans stand out like warts on witches' noses in the Fairy Kingdoms.'

'There's no time to waste,' Jesse said, taking the bag from Cathal and shoving it back into the pocket of her Forever Fitting Jeans. 'Let's hurry to the wood. We can enter the fairy ring in the clearing.'

As they stood up and hurried out onto the road, they didn't see the warlock, Kildrith. He was dark, not black but sinister and strangely irregular. He grimaced like a pouting monkey and narrowed his eyes. He was dressed in storm coloured clothes, although there was no sign of thunder or lightning. The brim of his wide hat was black. It shaded his ape-like face. He slipped his hand inside his long black coat, searching, delving so deeply that it appeared his secret body was a vast treasure chest. He was horribly out of place on that bitter cold morning.

Kneeling now he pulled his hand from his chest and threw the small metal box on the road, uttering mystical words of fantasy. He whispered magical lines never heard by human ears. He gripped the box in his clawed hands and pulses of blue light passed from him into it. In a flash, the shining box flew off ahead of him, humming like a bee, rotating at a tremendous speed towards its target.

Kildrith stood up and twisted in upon himself, folding like paper into a blue grey mist. Blending with the shadows, he silently stalked them.

Further down the road, something shuddered in the sewer. The manhole cover flipped open as if a penny had been tossed into the air. It twirled round and round and round until at last it rested in peace on the tarmac. What looked like gnarled and bony fingers slowly slithered out of the black hole, followed by the shadow of a beast that was tall and thin and unspeakably ugly.

Without sound it pursued Jesse, Cathal, and Kildrith towards the fairy ring.

When Jesse and Cathal reached the wood it was difficult to find the clearing. It was pitch dark and the narrow winding pathways were almost impossible to see. The only sound came from their footfalls, crunching the frosty undergrowth. Eventually, they found the clearing, as their eyes grew more accustomed to the dark. But they could not find the fairy ring. It was as if it had never existed.

'Where is it?' Jesse wanted to know.

'I don't know,' Cathal admitted. 'This has never happened to me before.'

'Are there other fairy rings that you know about?'

'Yes, but they're not in Millburn.'

'Where is the closest one?'

'Rainley.'

'Rainley? That's miles away.'

'Twenty miles by car,' Cathal said.

'But we haven't got a car,' Jesse pointed out.

'We'll have to go back to the house. I left my

purse in the kitchen. We need money to get a taxi into Rainley.'

There was a strange twinkle in Jesse's eye.

'What is it?' Cathal asked.

'We could be there in no time at all if you-'

'Jesse, that's not a good idea. Any kind of magic, including shape-shifting, performed in the human world leaves a scent, a tell-tale smell that would be easy to follow. If you live in the human world, then you have to play by human rules.'

'Really?'

'Really. It's a hard lesson, I know. But it's for the best. Remember, it was the ancient fairy people's magic that got us into bother with the humans in the first place.'

'But, Mum-'

'No means no, Jesse. We'll just have to do it the human way. No more arguments, please.'

'But, Mum,' Jesse said, nodding frantically behind Cathal.

'That's quite enough, from you, young lady,' Cathal said firmly.

'But, Mum. Look! I think we might have to break the rules ... and fast!'

The spinning, buzzing metal box Kildrith had sent ahead of him whizzed past Cathal's right ear. Jesse ducked, as the box plunged at her head. It stopped for a moment, hovering close by. It throbbed a vivid electric blue. Jesse gulped in horror as dozens of needle-sharp spikes appeared from each face. The mini robot was ready to do battle.

'Do something, Mum,' Jesse urged. 'NOW!'

Emerging from the dense wood into the clearing, strode the dark warlock, Kildrith. In his right hand he raised his wand, which shuddered with an enormous blue flaming energy. A bolt of lightning flashed out of the tip and scorched Jesse's cheek, crashing into a mighty oak tree to her left. The tree burst into flames.

Jesse yelled in pain and clutched her cheek.

'Death to the Soothsayers!' Kildrith raged, firing another bolt of lightning from his wand.

Jesse and Cathal dived to the ground as the sizzling bolt narrowly missed their heads. It hit a tree stump with a deafening crash, and the stump began to burn.

'Run!' Cathal shouted, dragging Jesse to her feet.

The box plummeted towards them, its spinning spikes gleaming in the light of the burning trees.

'There's nowhere to run to!' Jesse cried. 'Do something now!'

Driven by her fear, Jesse started to run anyway. As she reached the opposite side of the clearing, stumbling and sliding to keep her footing, she was grabbed hard from behind. She screamed in terror as she was lifted high into the air, legs and arms flailing wildly. Higher and higher she was carried, away from the burning wood and away from danger.

'It's all right, Jesse,' the great dragon said. 'We're safe for the time being.'

Jesse breathed a huge sigh of relief as she climbed on to her mother's ridged back. 'That was close,' she said, holding her wounded cheek.

'Maybe next time I ask you to break the rules you'll listen.'

'I'll make sure I do,' Cathal said. 'I promise.'

Three

Over the
Trip-Trap Bridge

'Look out for the churchyard, on the outskirt's of Rainley,' Cathal said, as they approached the patchwork of lights below them.

They had been flying for almost twenty minutes above the dark fields, crossing roads and train tracks, stands of trees, and the odd small village. They hadn't flown too high, because it was a bitterly cold night. Cathal had explained that the higher you flew the colder it became. She also wisely pointed out that whoever was chasing them would find it harder to spot them if they stayed low. Every few minutes Jesse glanced over her shoulder, certain that their pursuer would be right behind them, transformed into a giant and hideous flying beast. But she had spotted no-one.

'Is this it?' Jesse asked, as they landed. Row upon row of silhouetted gravestones stretched out all around them. 'This is really spooky.'

Cathal transformed into her human self, and said, 'There's a reason that this fairy ring is situated here. It doesn't take you to the Good Kingdom of Troth, but to Loath Town in the Dark Kingdom of Finnigull.'

'Is that close to Dendrith's Castle?'

'I'm sorry to say that it's too close for comfort - about four miles from the main gate.'

Jesse shook her head. The thought of Dendrith was a most unwelcome one.

'Hurry,' Cathal said, taking Jesse's hand. 'There's no time to waste.'

They ran along the maze of pathways which criss-crossed the thousands of graves. Jesse tried hard not to look at the gravestones, or the deep dark shadows around them. Her mind kept returning to her encounter with the ghosts of the dead giants, the Spriggans. It was an experience she did not wish for again.

A few minutes later, they reached the far end of the churchyard. There was a plot of grassland earmarked for future graves. In the corner, near a huge yew tree, Jesse could just make out a fairy ring in the coarse short grass. Around its circumference grew the tell-tale sign:

field mushrooms. She could also see something else.

'There's an amber haze,' she said. 'It's in the shape of a circle.'

'Your fairy vision is well-developed in one so young,' the dark figure said, appearing from behind the yew tree. 'I am impressed. And you, Cathal Jameson, or should I say, Cathal de Lacjard, are a magnificent shape-shifter if ever I saw one. You're dragon was to die for. And I, my dear child, have seen and destroyed many.'

The figure laughed insanely.

Cathal instinctively stood between her daughter and the warlock. 'Who are you and why do you want to kill us?'

'My name is Kildrith, and I will kill you because it's my work.'

'You mean you're paid. You're an assassin,' Cathal said disdainfully. 'Who paid you to kill us?'

'Who do you think?' Kildrith teased. 'Have a guess. Go on. You may be surprised.'

'No thanks,' Cathal said. 'We don't play games with killers.'

Kildrith pushed back his wide brimmed hat, revealing skin so thin that Jesse thought she could see his brain pulsating inside his skull.

'Pity,' he said, the tip of his wand beginning to glow. 'I love playing games. Hide and seek - now that's my favourite. Why don't you run and hide. I'll count to fifty without peeking. One, two, three ...'

'Run like the clappers!' Jesse yelled, turning on her heel as she emptied the contents of the two bags of Short-Fused Charms. From one bag fell thousands of tiny seeds, and from the other a multitude of tiny teeth.

Cathal needed no second telling. She, too, turned and ran back towards the church, grabbing Jesse's hand and leading the way.

First, there was a fizzing sound, as if a giant bottle of lemonade had been opened. Then, a second sound, a kind of low mad singing, followed by a series of ear-shattering bangs! A flash of white-blue light lit up the entire churchyard, and Jesse glanced behind her to see Kildrith flying backwards into the yew tree. Instead of being knocked unconscious, the warlock howled wildly and transformed into a huge snarling wolf.

There was a momentary silence. Then, emerging from the ground where Jesse had tossed the seeds and teeth, there appeared thousands of tiny replicas of the Gobbit, Iggywig. They were just eight inches tall, with faces so squashed they looked as if they had been smashed by a hammer. Their eyes glared madly. They had yellow caps on their heads, and wore strange luminous golden armour. They wielded battle-axes made from dragon's teeth. Instead of forming ranks, as Roman soldiers might have done, they attacked with an insane pandemonium.

Kildrith howled in pain as they slashed and cut, leaping onto his back, surrounding him. The vast numbers of ferocious tiny Gobitts surprised the warlock, whose snapping and biting proved little defence.

Jesse and Cathal stopped their withdrawal and watched in amazement as Kildrith was forced to retreat, ducking and diving between gravestones and monuments. Hurrying to the fairy ring, they couldn't resist the opportunity which presented itself. Producing a small plastic bottle from her coat pocket, Cathal gave Jesse some Time Stopper potion and took some herself.

As she stepped into the ring, Jesse turned to glimpse the transforming Kildrith but he, the battling Gobbits, and the churchyard vanished from her sight.

They emerged not in the beautiful mountainous Kingdom of Troth, but in the foul and disgusting town of Loath. Jesse recalled how Iggywig had once described it while they had journeyed high over Finnigull on the back of a Griffin. What was it he had said? Ah, yes, '... *tis an evil place a-full of dark deeds and miserable creatures.'*

Jesse did not doubt it.

They were standing in the ramshackle quarter of Loath on the western side of the town. The streets were made from thick slushy mud. Deep wheel tracks had created huge puddles everywhere they cared to look. A multitude of hoof, claw and paw prints were sunk into the mud, too. Jesse didn't recognise any of the prints, but her mind imagined all kinds of gruesome monsters and beasts that had made them.

Dawn's first light was just piercing the dark, and it was pouring with rain. There was no sound except for the single toll of a bell somewhere, and no sign of life. There were no birds singing. A terrible stench filled their nostrils. It smelled like rotten fish and onions. It seemed to be coming from everywhere.

Jesse gazed around. Unlike most of Alisbad City the buildings here were run down and derelict. Instead of being built from fine sandstone or marble, the houses which lined the closely packed streets were made from rotting wood and weather-beaten mud. They were mostly domed affairs, with long, thin slots for windows, and tiny doors covered with flaps of filthy leather. However, there were some taller buildings that were dotted about at random that rose forty feet high. Most of them leaned precariously, looking as if they were about to collapse. They, too, were made from wood and mud, and a few had faded signs above their doors: *Big Bad Bald Gnomes Liquor Store*, and *Aunt Magdrith's Woolly Vest Shop*, and *Dead Bob's Bats' Wing Take Away*. All the windows were shuttered or boarded up, with signs which read: *Keep Out! Enter at your own risk!* Or the most sinister of all - *Come on in - NEVER see daylight again!*

'Now what?' Jesse asked, looking for somewhere to shelter from the downpour.

'I'm not sure,' Cathal said, pulling her collar up around her neck. 'Let's find shelter first. This rain is burning my skin.'

As Jesse hurried as best she could through the sticky thick mud, she also felt the rain's burning effects. It was as if the rain was acid. Maybe that was why the streets were deserted, Jesse wondered. Acid rain!

A few moments later they reached one of the crooked tall buildings. Cautiously, they pushed open the rickety door and peered inside. There was a wide hall with a large fireplace in the middle. A wood fire smouldered, a spiralling green smoke rising towards charred rafters, seeking a way out through a hole in the roof. They sneaked through the hall and entered another room, much smaller and darker. Ahead, at the far end of the room, was a strange sight: no wall - just a bright blue wooden gate and a small picket fence.

'That's odd,' Jesse said, sensing something was wrong.

'It looks freshly painted,' Cathal said, edging a little closer to confirm her suspicion.

'What's a bright blue fence and gate doing in a place like this?'

'I don't know, but look out there,' Cathal

said, pointing beyond the gate to a beautiful garden, bathed in warm sunshine. 'The rain has stopped, thank goodness. How wonderful! It looks so inviting.'

'Glamour,' Jesse whispered. 'It has to be. Careful, Mum. Don't get too close.'

But it was too late.

Cathal pushed open the creaking gate and stepped in to the garden. Jesse hurried after her. This felt terribly wrong, terribly out of place. It had to be a glamour, some evil witch or warlock's illusion.

The garden was full of beautiful wild flowers, which gave off the most wonderful aromas. A small sparkling stream meandered through the lush garden. The sound of gurgling water was most comforting. Under a vine-clad pergola, and over a narrow trip-trap bridge, Jesse could see a wooden bench. She had an overwhelming urge to sit on the bench. Without any further thought she followed her mother and they sat down together, looking at the gate and fence and darkened room from which they had come.

From the shadows appeared, one by one, an awful sight. Some of the creatures were no more than two feet tall, while others were so high that they were stooping to fit in the room. If they had stood up to their full height their heads and shoulders would have smashed through the roof. Some crawled on all fours, yet others still skulked on two legs.

There were thin bony creatures, with many large black insect eyes, and fat hairy creatures with great protruding teeth and drool running from misshapen mouths. Then there were the Beastbots: part beast and part robot, where steel, titanium, and micro-chip had been merged with flesh and bone.

One Beastbot jerked forward out of the gloom and stopped abruptly halfway across the bridge. It was about ten feet tall, broad and muscular in the places where flesh could be seen instead of steel and titanium body parts. Most of its ghoulish features were covered by a black metal helmet, but one large black, almond-shaped eye glared without blinking. It raised its hydraulic lance and cutter, so that they were directed at Jesse and Cathal. In its third hand, (its flesh and bone one) it tossed a heavy-looking metal object that resembled an evil bowling ball.

'Why are you here?' the Beastbot asked in a cold metallic voice.

'We were sheltering from the rain,' Cathal explained. 'This was the first place we came to.'

'Why are you here?' the Beastbot repeated.

'I just answered your question. My answer hasn't changed.'

'Why are you here?'

More creatures came out of the darkness

and gathered around the Beastbot. They were all very ugly and sinister, carrying all manner of weapons. They mumbled in a garbled language neither Cathal nor Jesse understood. Some simply growled viciously, showing brown teeth, or snake-like tongues.

Jesse thought that they seemed either extremely angry or extremely hungry. Whatever, she wished she was somewhere far away.

'Why are you here?'

'Why are you here?' Cathal echoed back.

The Beastbot raised the ball above its head.

'Mum, why did you do that?' Jesse asked. 'I think you've upset it.'

'Why are you-'

'Oh, please!' Cathal shouted at the Beastbot. 'You're beginning to get on my nerves. Either hurl that thing or put it down and give your arm a rest! It must weigh a tonne.'

The creatures spoke all at once in their strange language, and began to push each other. A couple of them prodded one another with blades and axes. Some began to fight, growling and snarling and hissing.

'I don't like this,' Jesse said. 'It's getting out of hand.'

'Agreed,' Cathal said, the creatures' attentions swung quickly on them as they stood up from the bench. 'All of a sudden, this garden doesn't seem to be quite as attractive as it was a few moments ago. Let's get out of here.'

'Why are you here?' the Beastbot said stupidly, as it was trampled under foot, hoof, and paw by scores of stampeding creatures.

As Cathal gathered Jesse in her arms and began to shape-shift, the trip-trap bridge collapsed. The weight of the creatures was just too much, and they plunged into the stream, shrieking, as whatever it was beneath the water sucked them under and devoured them whole. Screaming small monsters with one eye and puffed out cheeks; howling massive monsters with fangs and talons biting and swiping; crying dark troll-like creatures whose skin was scaled and wart-riddled - all of them perished in a matter of seconds. Those who could, turned and leapt back into the dark room, melting into the shadows. But there were very few who escaped with their lives.

'Why ... are ... you ... here?' a metallic voice gurgled as its outstretched lance and cutters and ball sank beneath the foaming water.

The trip-trap bridge had gone, and Jesse and Cathal were left all alone on the other side of the stream.

But they were not alone for long.

Jesse drew in a sharp breath at the dark silhouette by the gate. Standing half in shadow and half out, the figure did not have to speak or raise his wide-brimmed black hat which covered his face for Jesse to know that it was Kildrith.

He seemed unwilling to step fully into the light of the garden, saying nothing. His cold breath rose like steam from a boiling kettle.

At last he spoke:

'The Jamesons.'

His voice was bitter, and slurred.

'How nice for you both - a garden of no escape,' he said sarcastically. 'It will make a fine resting place.'

'Why don't you join us in the sunshine?' Cathal said, ignoring his comments. 'You look as if you could do with some sun.'

At this, great clouds of steam rose angrily from his lips. He shifted back further into the shadows, his face a pale ball in the gloom.

'Mum, please don't wind him up,' Jesse urged. 'He looks angry enough already.'

'Trust me,' Cathal whispered, putting her hand across her mouth so that Kildrith couldn't hear. 'I know exactly what I'm doing.'

'Oh, good,' Jesse said, ironically. 'I'm glad someone does. Let's get out of here before this turns nasty.'

'Come on, Kildrith,' Cathal baited. 'It'll do you the world of good. Step into the sunshine.'

'That is not possible, as well you know, Cathal Jameson,' Kildrith snarled.

'Oh? Why not? Haven't you brought your

sunblock?'

At this, the wide-brimmed hat rose, untouched by Kildrith. The sight now revealed was enough to make Jesse feel sick. The Short-Fused Charm's effects had been devastating. Kildrith's face was a maze of wounds and scars, a face ruined like small smashed windows.

'You will pay for this,' Kildrith said in a cold, evil voice. 'And your slow pain will be my ever-lasting pleasure.'

In his right hand he lifted his wand, which ignited with a blue flaming energy. A bolt of lightning shot out of the tip, and Jesse and Cathal dived into a border of waist-high flowers. The lightning struck the bench with such force that it exploded into thousands of burning splinters.

Jesse covered her face as she rolled deeper into the flowerbed. Cathal was leading the way, crawling on her elbows, body close to the earth like a slithering snake. A bolt of lightning crashed into a tree trunk just ahead of them. It burst into flames, as they scampered around it, hurrying deeper into the garden.

'Stand and fight!' Kildrith shouted from the darkness. 'Show yourselves! Cowards!'

Jesse and Cathal kept as low as they could, feeling slightly more secure with every step away from the dark warlock. They knew they were no match for his lethal magic.

Suddenly something whizzed over their heads and landed in the soft earth with a dull thud just a few feet away.

It was then that they heard with growing horror the tick-tock, tick-tock of the small bomb. It was matt black, and reminded Jesse of a pimply golf ball.

Two more landed close by on the other side of them.

'Run!' Cathal yelled. 'Stay down as low as you can!'

Jesse followed her past the first bomb as it stopped ticking.

Click ... click ... whir!

Now was the time to get up and run for their lives. They sprinted as fast as their legs and adrenaline would carry them, deeper and deeper into the garden, which was now becoming more formal, with lawns and topiary figures and square herb gardens confined in low box hedges.

The explosion was deafening. Even though they were thirty yards away, the blast bowled them across one of the lawns like croquet balls. Broken branches, and ripped bark whooshed around them, followed a split second later by uprooted flowers and shrubs and clods of earth. A thorny bush scratched Jesse's face as it flew past at great speed, leaving two cuts on her cheek which looked like an equals sign.

Shaken, they scrambled to their feet and

fled into a luscious meadow. They did not stop or turn to glimpse Kildrith, but they could hear his curses. They were evil curses, the kind of which only a seething warlock could issue. They had escaped - just.

Beneath his cursing came a deep destructive sound. It was a sound they wished they had not heard. The Rumble was closing in, not only on them, but on all the inhabitants of Loath Town.

Four

Dragon Cove

The beauty of the landscape did not diminish as they strode through meadows and skirted small woodlands. It was pleasantly warm and bees and butterflies busied themselves on the abundance of wild flowers. After an hour or so they stopped to rest by a pebble-dashed brook. All around them were orchards, apple, pear, and plum, as well as orchards the like of which Jesse had never seen. Even though it was November, the trees were sagging with the weight of the ripe fruit.

'That one looks so delicious,' Jesse said, reaching up to pick the yellow and purple striped fruit. 'What's it called?'

'A slow-death malgrim,' Cathal said, picking a rosy red apple from a nearby tree and crunching it with delight. 'One bite of the malgrim and its juices begin a horrible slow-death that poisons the brain. Madness quickly follows an uncontrollable urge to bite every dog or cat in sight.'

Jesse laughed. 'You're joking, aren't you?'

'No,' Cathal said flatly. She tossed an apple to Jesse. 'Here. Eat this. Live to fight another day.'

'Tis a-wise wordings your mother be a-speaking,' said the creature behind them. 'Jesse be a-foolish to eat such a-disgusting poison.'

Jesse turned and squealed with joy. 'Iggywig!'

They hugged for a long time.

'Jesse be a-using the Short-Fused Charm in the human world?' Iggywig said at last, holding her at arm's length.

'Yes, how do you know that?'

'Short-Fused Charm be a-sending a little mini-me as soon as it be a going bang! Mini-Gobitt be a-rudely interrupting Iggywig's snoozing. His dragon-tooth axe be a-very hurtful weapon.'

He yawned widely, showing his toothless gums. 'Be very sleepy now.'

'Do you know how we can find our way out

of this place?' Cathal asked. 'I'm concerned that we should be on our way as quickly as possible. We need to find somewhere safe to rest, to eat properly, and to plan our next move.'

'Tis a good fortune that Iggywig be a-loaded with the means and know-how to be a-granting all that you be a-wishing.' He clicked his fingers three times and three hessian sacks appeared from thin air. He handed one each to Jesse and Cathal without an explanation. 'Come - follow, if you be a-pleasing. The Gravitunnel be a-close by.'

'What's a Gravitunnel?' Jesse asked.

'Tis a surprise you be a-liking.'

They snaked a mile or more along the bank of the winding brook. At last they reached a curious hole in the ground. It was just wide enough for one person to slip in to. And that is exactly what the Gobitt did.

'Tis a-thrilling worth all the stories in Kayblade's head,' he said, leaping into the hole. 'Be a-seeing you on the other side. Yeeaah!'

'Don't be in such a hurry, Jesse,' Cathal said, grabbing Jesse's hand as she prepared to jump. 'Shall we share a sack? Ride the Gravitunnel together? It'll be safer that way.'

'It's all right, Mum,' Jesse said, smiling. 'I'll be fine on my own. This looks like fun!'

'Listen to me - carefully. If for some reason we get separated, make your way to the Knoll of

Knowing. All right?'

'Yes, Mum,' Jesse said. She knew when her mother was worried. Now was a time to listen. 'If we get separated, I'll go to the Knoll.'

'Good girl,' Cathal said, kissing her daughter's forehead. 'Bon-voyage!'

'Yahoo!' Jesse yelled, as she jumped into the hole, riding the sack as if she'd just begun to descend a fairground helter-skelter.

Down and down and down she slid. The rushing wind blew her hair out in a long veil behind her, and stung her eyes. The tunnel was narrow and dark and smelly, and she kept banging her elbows on the metal sides. After a few minutes, the thrill of plummeting into the unknown subsided, for she suddenly realised with a shocking horror that she had no idea how far she would have to plunge. She also had no idea where she was going. It was now that she wished she had shared a sack with her mother. She was very scared.

The deeper she travelled into the Gravitunnel, the colder it became, until her hands and face were numb. Then, when she thought she couldn't stand it any longer, the twisting and turning, bumping and hurtling around and around got worse. Like a corkscrew rollercoaster, the ride became faster and faster. She banged her head so many times she thought that she would be knocked unconscious at any moment. Her heart thumped madly in her chest, as she gasped for breath. Her mouth was terribly parched. She refused to open her eyes, because to do so made her feel awfully sick. And the nerve-racking sound of bone against metal was grinding her down.

Then, suddenly, she began to slow and rise.

Up and up and up she rose, until her speed was snail pace. Now this was more like it, she thought. All the danger of the ride had gone. She had time to relax and enjoy. Although it was dark, her eyes had grown accustomed to it. She could now make out complex designs and simple drawings on the wall of the tunnel. They shone magically in the dark. There were scenes of battles, and feasts, and hunts, and great celebration. Some drawings showed armies of magicians fighting with charms and magic. Everywhere she saw strange symbols and glyphs. Wild beasts - especially dragons - were depicted in almost every drawing.

Eventually, at the highest point, she stopped. But her sense of relief was short-lived, because below her the tunnel dropped away steeply. The ride was not over. The downhill nightmare was about to begin again.

It came out of the blue. Something inside her head told her to wait. It made sense. Her mother would be here soon. Yes, they could ride together. The prospect cheered her up no end.

The near vertical drop into the gloom didn't seem so bad after all.

A few minutes later, Cathal cruised into view. Despite the mirk, Jesse could see that she looked extremely pale and shaken.

'Oh, thank goodness, you are all right,' Cathal said. 'That was absolutely awful.'

'I know, Mum,' Jesse echoed. 'I hope you're ready to do it all over again?'

The little colour that was left in Cathal's face drained like water down a plug hole as she peered into the steepness of the tunnel.

'It won't be so bad now that we can travel together,' Jesse offered.

Cathal put on a brave face, somehow managing a smile.

'Come on,' she said. 'Let's not think about it - just take the plunge.'

They organised the sacks so that they were sitting on both of them, Jesse tucked in between Cathal's legs. Just as they were about launch themselves into the abyss, they heard the metallic swish and bang of another rider. Someone was behind them, closing in fast. Turning to each other, they whispered:

'Kildrith.'

They needed no second bidding. Suddenly the nightmare of the tunnel didn't seem so bad after all. They slid over the edge and screamed as they dropped.

One heart-stopping sack-ride later they emerged from the tunnel next to the Gobitt. Jesse wasn't sure who to kiss first now that she'd survived. For most of the journey she had been sure she wouldn't live to breathe fresh air again. But here she was, standing next to a sign which read:

Dragon Cove –
Decent, honest, law-abiding folk
turn back while you still have
a chance. Smugglers, pirates,
politicians, estate agents,,
and used-car salesmen
most welcome.

The back street dead end they were in was deserted, but for two cat-like creatures who were snuffling around discarded dustbins. When they saw Jesse and Iggywig appear from the hole, their hair stood up on end, making them look the size of a large dog. Hissing crossly at being disturbed from their scavenged morsels, they scurried away around the corner.

'Savacats,' Iggywig said under his breath. 'Be a-sneaky pest, best not to be a-stroking unless you be a-wanting the Savacat-scratch fever. Vicious beasts!'

The Gobbit clicked his fingers and pointed at the hole. From his fingertips, rivers of gold and blue sparks flew out. A small blue-gold bubble of spinning light covered the hole.

'What did you do?' Jesse asked.

'Tis a Light-lock that be a-stopping uninvited guests,' he said, swirling his kaleidoscope eyes for effect. 'Tis time to be a-hurrying.'

Turning the corner, Jesse gazed along the narrow dusty alley and was amazed by the sight which greeted her. The myriad shops here were packed tightly together, some with their own hand-written sign above the shop door or window. There was *Honest Handsome Herbert's Home-brew*, a shop filled with every wine, spirit and beer 'known to carry a kick like a mule.' They passed by *Guns Galore, Ammo Aplenty* where a gang of tough-looking elves were huddled in a darkened corner, mumbling and looking around suspiciously. Then there was *Jem's Jewellery Jamboree*, a tiny shop that had a thick iron grid on the window where enormous diamonds and gemstones sparkled. Many of the shops were anonymous, dingy affairs, where Jesse spied shifty-looking dwarves and goblins and pixies making shady deals together.

'Tis not wise to be a-hanging around on the alley,' the Gobbit warned. He nodded towards

Ulek's *Refuge For Ruffians and Rogues.* 'We be a-needing to rest at Ulek's. He be a-expecting us.'

Jesse wasn't sure she liked the sound of *Ulek's Refuge For Ruffians and Rogues*, but as she crossed the threshold to be greeted by the twelve feet tall giants, Ulek, his wife, his grandmother, his sister, her two tiny sons, and Ulek's dozen eight feet tall children, all of her fears evaporated.

'Ah, welcome to Ulek's, Jesse Jameson!' Ulek bellowed, hugging her in his huge arms like a long lost relative. He was part troll, part giant, and part ogre mixed breed. He was plump and very ancient, judging by the deep wrinkles that creased his face. He was wearing baggy blue breeches, a baggy green lumberjack shirt, a filthy full-length apron, and enormous black buckled boots. On every one of his thick podgy fingers he wore gold rings. His eyes were as dark and shiny as polished coal, and his smile was as warm as a fire. 'Your name is legend in these parts,' he went on. 'And I won't embarrass you by asking you to tell us one of your magnificent stories. We all know that Brimbalin has the rights to them - although, like you, we feel his price was extremely high in return for so little. Still, mustn't grumble, eh? Or maybe we should?'

At this, all of Ulek's family cheered and laughed, and Jesse and Cathal were jostled into the large banqueting hall at the rear of the building. There were flaming torches on the walls, and the great height of the hall made Jesse feel a little dizzy as she looked up to the vaulted ceiling. In the centre was a mosaic of a dragon's head.

Jesse was seated at the right side of Ulek, and Cathal on his left at the head of the table. These seats were deemed a great honour in Ulek's family, and he told them so - at least a hundred times as they ate and drank and drank and ate until they could eat and drink no more.

'So, to business,' Ulek said, as the great table was cleared by his very efficient children. He let out a mighty belch, and winked at Jesse. 'Good grub, eh?'

'Very,' Jesse said, trying to muster a belch herself.

'Er ... excuse me, Jesse,' Cathal said in firm tones. 'Where are your manners?'

Ulek let out another massive burp.

'What's in has to fly out,' he said, wiping his mouth on the back of his sleeve. 'Ain't that right, Grandma?'

The wizened old giant woman sitting next to Iggywig nodded, winked, and belched in the gobbit's face. Licking her wrinkled lips, she spat out her false teeth straight into Cathal's pewter goblet she still held in her hand. A ruby-coloured mead splashed everywhere. Everyone roared with laughter, except Cathal, who was not amused. She slammed the goblet down on the chunky oak table wishing she were some place else.

'I think it's time we were going,' Cathal said. 'Thank you for your hospitality.'

'But, Mum-'

'Don't be leaving on my account, deary,' Grandma said. 'It's just a bit of harmless fun. I'm always making a fool of myself at the expense of others, ain't that right, Ulek?'

'Always, Grandma,' Ulek said, smiling. He turned to Cathal and his face became deadly serious. 'You seek two humans - one an adult, the other a boy, I hear?'

'Yes,' Cathal said, straining to hear above the din the rest of the family was now making. Tumbling dwarf acrobats and juggling elves skipped and ran around the hall. Fire-breathing pixies soon joined them. A band of minstrels played an old dance tune. The party was just beginning.

'The boy was found by a bunch of trooping fairies in Troth. I hear he was in good health, but terribly homesick. The last I heard, they were riding towards the Land of Unfulfilled Dreams in the north. He slipped out of their camp one night but was caught by grey goblins. They set him to work in their mines.'

'Was his name Jake Briggs?' Jesse asked,

great concern in her voice.

'More than I have told, I don't know, Jesse Jameson. But I do know the whereabouts of your dad, Roger Jameson.'

'Where is he?' Cathal asked eagerly.

'Is he all right?' Jesse wanted to know.

'Is he with the Scratchits?'

'Has Dendrith imprisoned him in her despicable dungeons?'

'Is he in Loath Town?'

'Oh, tell us he's safe and well and-'

Jesse's jaw dropped wide, for being led by Iggywig through the cheering crowd of Ulek's family was her Dad and Roamer. She and Cathal ran swiftly into his open arms and they swung around and around for a long time.

The story Roger Jameson told was brief and puzzling. They were gathered around a roaring log fire in a smaller room just off the great hall, where comfortable giant green sofas and chairs were jammed with Ulek's giant family. They listened intently, hanging on to every word. After all, it might not be a legendary Jesse Jameson story, but it was her father, Roger, who spoke of being glamoured so deeply that he couldn't remember a single moment of his time with the Scratchits.

'I don't even remember the trade,' the bewildered Roger said. He was a tall, slender man of forty, with silver flecks in his blond hair. His sparkling blue eyes reflected the flickering flames as he sat with his arms around Jesse and Cathal. Roamer was snuggled up in front of the fire, snoring.

'Then I'll tell the rest of tale, for it was Ulek who made the trade under the direction of my good friend, Iggywig,' Ulek said. He guzzled down his huge goblet of mead, and signalled for one of his children to bring more. 'Now then ... it's a tale not of heroic rescues, or challenging quests, but a good old-fashioned smugglers' trading tale.'

His family applauded and toasted his health, swigging back more mead. To Jesse, it seemed that the crowd had doubled at least. She didn't recognise many of the faces. She wondered just how many members there were of Ulek's family. She guessed there were about fifty crammed into the room, and more were squeezing in through the door at the back.

'I had heard through the ... er ... grapevine,' Ulek carried on, 'that the Scratchits were bored of the glamoured human they had in tow ...' He glanced across at the Jamesons. 'I apologise for some of my people's attitudes to glamoured humans, but if the truth be told ... we think any human stupid enough to be glamoured deserve all they get.'

The Jamesons nodded, and Roger glowed

red a little.

'Anyway, the Scratchits came, as all bargain-hunters come, to Dragon Cove. This place has a rotten reputation of wheeling and dealing. If you want to sell, or get rid of stolen goods, then there's always some rogue waiting to buy, or rip you off, as long as the price is right.

'The Scratchits were waiting for me in *Slippery Sid's Snakeskin Shop*, just off Dragon High Street. It was difficult at first to spot them, because the place was crawling with hags and witches and warlocks. Seems they buy all their potion stuff at Sid's. Anything that has scales or fur or claws on it, then Sid's the Sylph to get it, by means foul and fair. But mainly foul.

'In a dingy corner of the shop, with a clear glass barrel of spiders to my left, and a tank of live wriggling snakes to my right, I met the Scratchits ...'

"Gimme that handbag!" the twin called Judy bawled.

"Get lost, yer smelly tartlet," Trudy yelled back, yanking on the snakeskin bag. "I saw it first."

"No yer didn't. I did. It's mine, pig-breath!"

"Mine!"

"No, mine, skunk mouth!"

"Get lost!"

"No, you get lost!"

'I've never seen such ugly over-dressed teenagers in all my life,' Ulek said. He shivered at the thought of them. 'Revolting!'

'So what happened next, Uncle?' a child said from the crowd.

Ulek shook his head. 'I met the disgusting Claris Scratchit.' He turned to Jesse. 'How you ever put up with her I'll never know. She was so rude!'

"What are you gawking at?" Claris Scratchit had said to me.

"I hear you have a human to trade," I had said, ignoring her insult.

"What's it to you, dog's breath?" Judy Scratchit had butted in.

"Yeh, what's it to you?" Trudy Scratchit echoed.

"Maybe, I'm buying, if you're selling."

"Maybe, we ain't selling," Judy Scratchit said, curling her top lip like Elvis. "Maybe, we are."

"We'll think about it," Claris Scratchit said coldly. "Meet us at *Matilda's Magic Market* at midnight. Now push off, before we change our minds."

'At midnight I ventured into Matilda's, a tiny shop that wasn't a market at all. There were rows of shelves stacked from the floor to the ceiling. Neatly scrolled labels identified brightly coloured boxes which read: *Potions Most Painful; Spells Most Smelly; Charms Most Choking; Visions Most Vicious; Short-Fused Charms; Body Bits - Old and New; Dark Glamours Galore; Voodoo Vitamins; Raptures Most Riveting; Teleportation Tips - How to keep yourself together when all around you are falling apart; Chameleon Sweets; Pendulums Most Pricey; Crystal Ball Bargains ...* The list was endless.

"Hello? Is there anybody there?" I called.

'There was no sign of Matilda.'

'An evil-looking cat waltzed by, carrying a dead rat in its mouth. Seconds later, Judy and Trudy Scratchit ambled in to the shop and said: "Good boy, Darth-V. Clever boy, catching a rat."

'Claris Scratchit stood in the doorway, with Roger Jameson dutifully standing behind her. His eyes were vacant.'

"Sorry we're late," Claris Scratchit said without meaning it, "but my girls wouldn't leave the hotel without making themselves look beautiful, would you, girls?"

'They ignored their mother's comment and began to whinge,' Ulek said.

"We're really bored. Let's go clubbing. I want to go clubbing - right now!"

"All right, girls, choose something you fancy from Matilda's shop. Clubbing is no fun unless you've got magic to hand. We'll be going in a few minutes."

"I don't want this magic stuff. It's boring," Judy Scratchit moaned. "I'm bored with turning handsome frogs into ugly princes."

"Yeh, we're bored with turning dwarves into dragons, and elves into elephants. We want to go clubbing!"

"All right - all right. Let me sell your step-father first."

"You won't be able to give him away, he's so useless," Judy Scratchit said acidly. "Just look at him. He doesn't know what day it is, let alone his name."

'She sauntered across to Roger,' Ulek carried on, 'and patted his head like a puppy. His dog, Roamer, sat obediently next to him.'

"Diddum miss 'or ickle Jesse jerk face?" Judy said.

'Roger Jameson said nothing. The glamour was too deep.

'Bored with the game of whinging, the twins played with Darth-V's dead rat for awhile, then poked around the shop, while Claris named her price.'

"Five thousand Heckles, and not a Shindish more," she snarled.

"Four thousand Heckles and a phial of Old Mother Alice Spring's Olde Worlde gin and tonic water," I said.

"Four thousand, seven hundred and fifty

Heckles."

"Four thousand, two hundred."

"You drive a hard bargain, you ugly son of a dung beetle," she retorted. "Four and a half thousand and that's my final offer. And I'll throw in the scabby dog. Take it or leave it."

"Done."

"Done."

'We spat into the palm of our hands and patted each other on the cheek, as is the custom in Dragon Cove when striking a deal.'

Once the cheering and applauding, congratulating and back-patting had subsided, Jesse was glad to have been ushered to a cosy room at the top of Ulek's establishment. Roger and Cathal were shown to a slightly bigger room across the corridor. Next to Jesse (who had the comforting company of Roamer) Iggywig settled down for a well-earned sleep.

'Don't worry, Jesse Jameson,' Ulek had said before turning in himself. 'You are well protected here.' He nodded to a vicious-looking giant who would guard the corridor throughout the night. 'If you need anything at all – just ask young Viktor here. He'll make sure your every need is seen to.'

'Thank you,' Jesse said.

'Good night. Sleep well.'

But Jesse found it difficult to sleep. Even

though she was very happy to have her dad back again in one piece. For somewhere out there - all alone, forced to work in a goblin mine - was her best friend, Jake Briggs.

Five

The Goblin Mines

Jesse watched the tide going out in Alisbad Bay. It left rock pools speckled with barnacles. Crabs and urchins buried themselves just beneath the sodden sand. Starfish wallowed like pink pigs in rivulets and tiny pools of seawater.

Jesse felt free here. It reminded her of holidays with Mum and Dad on Southend beach. She loved to feel the softness of the dry sand on her bare feet. She had her trousers rolled up and was carrying her shoes, leaving small footprints in the sand, which were quickly filled with tiny drifts of sand blown by a gentle breeze.

'It's so peaceful here,' Cathal said.

'It's beautiful, Mum,' Jesse sighed.

They were either side of Roger Jameson, arms linked to his. It was early morning and the sun was low in the sky. Dragon Cove was a few hundred yards behind them, perched precariously on a cliff top. There was a maze of smugglers' tunnels dug into the red rock of the cliff-face. Iggywig was ahead of them, trying and failing to catch crabs from a rock pool. Beyond him, Jesse could see Island Gloom, a notorious island where smugglers met to deal in secret. And beyond the island the ocean rose and fell like a sleeping liquid giant deeply breathing.

'Your father and I have been talking,' Cathal said, as they sat on the sand, gazing out into the blue of sky and ocean. 'We need a long rest, time to get body and soul back together again. The effects of the prolonged glamour have taken their toll on your father. His memory is not what it used to be. It may take some time to heal. Peace and quiet - that's what he needs. We're returning with Roamer to the human world as soon as we can.'

Jesse's heart gave a horrible jolt. She gazed tearfully at the crashing waves. She knew what was coming next.

'Rather than force you to do something against your will,' Cathal went on, 'we think you're old enough to make up your own mind about whether you want to come back with us or stay here. Don't we, Roger?'

Roger Jameson was snapped from his reverie, a vacant place of comforting bright colours and soothing mystical words. 'Er ... yes ... what ever you say, love,' he managed.

Jesse was dumfounded. Had she heard her mother correctly? Did she say something about being old enough to make up her own mind?

'We'll leave it with you, Jesse,' Cathal said, picking up a small pebble and skimming it across the ocean's surface. 'All right?'

Jesse nodded, still dazed, and watched the pebble skid three times off the ocean, sinking without trace. What to do? Mum's words had really thrown her. She'd been expecting Mum and Dad to carry on with her, searching for Jake Briggs. But this ... this ... decision she'd been given made everything so much harder. An argument would have been better. She could have ranted on about all the reasons why she should continue the search for her best friend, even if they wanted to return to the human world.

Five minutes went by before she broke the serenity.

'I have to carry on here, Mum,' Jesse said at long last. 'As much as I want to come home with you and Dad, I can't. Jake is my best friend. I have to find him.'

'Tis a-pleasure Iggywig be a-helping Jesse,

too,' the Gobbit said, still trying to catch crabs from the rock pool. Even though he was twenty yards away, his hearing was extraordinarily good. 'Be a-finding your friend together?'

'Thank you,' Cathal said to the Gobbit. 'I know Jesse will be safe in your company.'

'Be as safe as a-bungalow in a storm.'

'As safe as houses, you mean,' Jesse corrected.

'Be a-knowing my houses from my bungalows, Jesse Jameson. Iggywig would a-rather be on the ground than a-high in the air when a hurricane be a-blowing!'

They all laughed as the Gobbit tumbled head over heels across the sand, clowning around, his kaleidoscope eyes spinning crazily. He clicked his fingers twice, and in his right hand appeared a rainbow-coloured flyboard. He threw it high into the air, but before hitting the beach it righted itself, stopping a foot from the sand. It purred like a contented kitten.

'Be a-waiting your commandings,' he said, leaping onto the flyboard. 'Be a-ready when you be, Jesse.'

'I'm ready,' Jesse said, climbing aboard.

Her parents didn't need to bend down to kiss her good-bye now that she had the flyboard to raise or lower her. As she and Iggywig hurtled around the bay, she thought it best not to look back, because the pain of seeing her parents waving might have been too much to bear. Instead, she focused on the task ahead: the rescue of Jake Briggs from the goblin mines.

Slowly, lowering themselves carefully with the ropes, they descended the shaft into the Goblin Mines. A few minutes later, they reached the bottom. The smallest noise sounded huge, reverberating around the maze of dark tunnels and caverns. Even their breathing echoed terribly.

As her eyes grew accustomed to the dark, Jesse could see that they were in a large cavern. At first she thought that they were alone. But then the cavern lit up, as if someone had magically thrown a switch.

It was lit by a great orange fire at the far end, and by small torches along the walls. It was packed with goblins. But these were not the kind of goblins Jesse had once encountered at Dendrith's Dungeons or in Alisbad or Dragon Cove. These were dirty, grey mining goblins, dressed in dirty grey tunics, and carrying huge serrated swords and pickaxes. They all chortled and hammered their weapons on the rock floor, clapping their hands with glee as Iggywig dropped down seconds later.

'Disgusting!' spat Whipflog, the fat, red-eyed goblin leader. His ears were pointed and he showed boar-like ivory tusks. He grimaced and flashed his needle-sharp teeth. 'A changeling and a Gobbit. How quaint.'

The hoards of goblins surrounding them laughed heartily, and slowly inched forward, snarling and gnashing teeth.

'What brings you to our humble abode? Fancy nicking our gold, do yer?' Whipflog growled.

''Tis not be our mission,' Iggywig said.

'Then what is? Just paying a friendly social call, eh?'

The hoards stamped their weapons on the hard rock floor, howling with laughter. There was a dark menace in their eyes which Jesse did not care for. These wild creatures frightened her badly.

'Er ... no ... we ... er ... are lost,' Jesse offered lamely. 'We are looking for a hu-'

'Humid place to be a-sleeping for the night,' Iggywig barged in, trying his best to lie convincingly. 'This child be a-needing lots of water.'

'Oh, dear, such a shame,' Whipflog mocked. 'Did you hear that brethren? These poor fairies are lost and need somewhere wet to sleep!'

'Shame!' cried the goblins.

'Pity!' yelled some more.

'We know exactly the place for you two,' Whipflog said, his black eyes narrowing to evil slits. 'Don't we brethren?'

'Aye!' yelled the hoards.

'Seize them!' Whipflog ordered. 'Chain them together, and take them to the north-eastern Deep Mine. Set them to work on the loading shift.'

'Aye!' yelled a dozen goblins, and they rushed in towards Jesse and the Gobbit.

Jesse tried to dodge the goblins but there were too many. She and Iggywig were over-powered in seconds, chained fast in minutes, and an hour later were thirsty, hungry, and extremely exhausted. The work they had been forced to do was not easy; loading gold dust with wide shovels onto carts that sped away on tiny rail tracks into a maze of tunnels.

'Work faster!' the goblin foreman ordered, and he poked anyone who seemed to be slacking; he also poked those he'd taken a disliking to with his axe no matter how hard they worked.

Jesse had never imagined such a horrid and degrading scene. All around her, frail and under-fed creatures shovelled gold dust into a stream of never-ending carts. Many of the creatures were old and thin and weak, some women, many children from every species of fairy she had ever seen or heard of. Everyone was linked together, so that a three foot length of heavy chain was all that separated them. When creatures collapsed from exhaustion, as they frequently did, a team of goblins quickly raced in, unlocked their chains, replaced them with other slaves, and dragged them unceremoniously away.

Jesse glanced around for the hundredth time but still could not see Jake Briggs. She couldn't hide her worry, but she had to keep thinking positively. Maybe he'd escaped? Or maybe Ulek's information was wrong? Maybe -

The flash of blinding light came without warning. The flaming torches along the walls of the tunnels went out, one by one, until all that could be seen was the occasional glow of slashing and cutting white light. Screams came and went. The slave creatures simply crouched or huddled in a ball, unable to move far. They didn't have the energy to cry out in fear. The grey goblins crashed into each other in the darkness, panicked by the surprise attack. They wielded their axes and swords, but did more damage to their own kind. Their attacker was fast, and brave, and seemed to be able to see as well in the dark as any creature could in daylight. It was an impossible fight and the goblins, who had managed to escape, scurried away into the depths of the mine, yelling for reinforcements.

The binding chains were easily cut as if they were butter by the sword of light. Hundreds of creatures were freed in minutes, and hurried away down the tunnels, issuing thanks and praise to the unseen emancipator. Jesse caught a glimpse of the figure as his sword of light flashed through her chains. She gazed briefly into his extraordinary eyes - like beacons of golden light. His nose was long and broad. His lips were full. He was human - no doubt.

'There is no time to talk,' he said in his low, powerful voice. 'Quickly. Follow me.'

The Dragon Hunter sped along the tunnels, with Jesse and Iggywig finding it hard to keep up the pace. He zig-zagged left, then right, then left and right at the cross-roads, until Jesse had lost count of all the twists and turns. Each time they came to the end of a tunnel, Iggywig clicked his fingers and pointed at it. From his fingertips, rivers of gold and blue sparks gushed out. A large blue-gold bubble of spinning light covered the tunnel like a transparent door.

'Tis no goblin I be a-knowing who will unpick my Light-locks,' he said, nodding in a satisfied voice.

Fifteen exhausting minutes later, they reached a small cavern. Jesse saw broken and discarded mining carts, rusty tools, and what looked like slumped skeletons of long dead slaves partially hidden in the shadows. Rising up from the cavern floor to its domed ceiling was a column of rock that reminded her of a giant apple core.

'Tis a wonderful sight for eyes that be asore,' Iggywig said. 'A Rokulator!'

'A what you later?' Jesse said.

'The Rokulator tis a fine transporting device that the goblins be a-using to get them from the top to the bottom.'

'But how?'

Jesse walked around the Rokulator, looking for an entrance. She tapped it cautiously with her forefinger. It felt solid and cold - just like ... well ... just like rock.

'We have no time for this discussion,' the Dragon Hunter said. 'Stand back.'

'The kind slayer be right, as a-usual,' Iggywig said. He put a bony finger to his ear. 'Tis an army of mad goblins me be a-hearing. They be a-wild with a-ragings! We better be a-hurrying fast.'

Jesse heard nothing except the rustle of parchment. The Dragon Hunter was unfolding a set of instructions. From the embarrassed look in his eyes, he was not at all comfortable with having to rely on a piece of parchment to tell him what to do next.

'Damn soothsayer,' he muttered under his breath. 'Now what do I say?'

'Tis a-pleasure for me to be a-helping, if I may, kind slayer,' Iggywig said, moving forward to peered at the parchment.

The Dragon Hunter rounded on the Gobitt, thrusting his face to within an inch of the

JESSE JAMESON AND the bogie beast

concerned little creature. 'If I need your help, then I'll ask for it, Gobchops!'

Iggywig backed away, shrugging. 'Be no offence meant, slayer. Iggywig just a-trying to lend a hand.'

Jesse heard them before she saw them, like stampeding buffalo, charging along the five tunnels that led into the cavern from different directions. Their echoing cries of revenge squeezed tightly in her stomach. They were closing in fast.

'Quickly,' she urged the Dragon Hunter, who was shaking his head despairingly at the words on the parchment. 'Before it's too late!'

'Rok ... ul ... at ... tor ... op ... en!'

Nothing happened.

'Rok ... ul ... at ... tor ... op ... en!'

Still nothing.

'Oh, hurry, please,' Jesse said frantically. 'Let Iggywig help.'

'Be pleased to,' Iggywig said. 'Iggywig good at a-speaking the ancient goblin talk. Human talk never be a-opening the Rokulator.'

'Rok ... ul ... at ... tor ... op ... en!'

Nothing.

'Rok ... ul ... at ... tor ... op ... en!'

'Oh, give me that here,' Jesse said, snatching the parchment out of the Dragon Hunter's hands. She glanced at the strange symbols:

'What the-' she began. She shoved the parchment into Iggywig's hands, nodding towards one of the tunnel entrances. 'Here, you might want to hurry.'

Whipflog emerged with his hoards of raging goblins. They snarled and spat and gnashed their thin needle-like teeth. They butted heads together like wild rams, locking tusks and howling. They didn't look happy.

'Rokulator - snargggumfff!' Iggywig shouted above the racket, and he slapped the rock hard.

Instantly, the rock opened like lift doors. The Dragon Hunter and Jesse hurried inside. Before joining them, Iggywig delved into his pocket, pulling out three small leather bags. He wrenched open the drawstrings and hurled the contents towards Whipflog's advancing goblins.

'Run like the clappers!' Iggywig yelled. He dived into the Rokulator. 'Rokulator - krabbsmagggumff!'

Just before the doors closed with a deafening crunch, Jesse saw the Short-Fused Charm explode. Emerging from the ground came thousands of tiny replicas of Iggywig. They wielded battle-axes made from dragon's teeth, yet there was one major difference from the creatures Jesse had unleashed on Kildrith: these replicas flew as fast as hummingbirds, slashing and thrusting their tiny weapons at the bewildered, retreating goblins.

The velocity at which the lift rose surprised Jesse. The Rokulator shook like a space shuttle taking off. Her stomach lurched. Feeling oddly as though her legs had turned to lead, she clung to the Dragon Hunter for support. Iggywig clung to Jesse, whimpering.

'Tis Iggywig's worst nightmare,' the Gobbit confessed. 'Be no a-liking heights!'

'Too late now,' the Dragon Hunter said, smiling.

Jesse thought she saw a strange delight in the Dragon Hunter's eyes. There was still no love lost between them.

Hardly daring to look at each other for fear of losing it totally, Jesse clung to the Dragon Hunter, and Iggywig to Jesse, until they stopped with a sudden jolt. Jesse felt her stomach somersault as the doors opened. The three of them spilled out into the sunshine to the wide-grinned greeting of a very happy, old, shape-shifting soothsayer.

'Your mother sent me a message last night,' Perigold explained, as he hugged Jesse. 'We thought you could do with some help.'

'We were doing just fine on our own, weren't we, Iggywig?' Jesse said, embarrassed at being captured.

Iggywig pulled a ridiculous face that was hard to read. 'Tis me who be a-glad to see you again, kind soothsayer. Tis not a place of work me be a-wishing on my worst enemy. The goblin mines be a place of great evil.'

Emerging from a mine shaft a few hundred yards away, they saw a dozen or so slaves. They shaded their eyes against the glare of the sunlight and scurried away in many directions - some heading east towards Alisbad, some north towards the Standing Stones, and a handful venturing west to the foot of the Mountains of Mourn. There was no sign of Jake - not a human amongst them.

'Jake was moved yesterday,' Perigold said, as if reading Jesse's mind.

'How do you kn-' Jesse began, but her sentence was sliced by more pressing concerns.

'We should be leaving,' the Dragon Hunter urged. 'The goblins will not give up a chase easily. Listen - I hear their dogs. We must go now.'

The baying goblin hounds were a terrible sound. As they swelled out of the mine's entrance, the sight of them gave Jesse a shock. The hounds were huge, gangly, drooling beasts that were twice the size of Irish wolfhounds. They had grey tangled fur hanging down to the ground and tiny, shiny red eyes. There were at least fifty of them in pursuit.

The Gobbit produced his flyboard and Perigold transformed into a black flying horse. The Dragon Hunter leapt onto Perigold's back, while Jesse joined Iggywig on the flyboard. It wasn't long before they were soaring high into the sky, leaving the howling hounds and fist-waving goblins in their wake.

Six

Mystic Mo's Crusty Crystal Ball

At the foot of the imposing Mountains of Mourn they headed towards a magnificent valley below. There was so much to ogle that Jesse didn't know what to look at first. There were thousands of fairy creatures wandering around an enormous fairground. From her dizzy height, she spied thirteen giant Ferris wheels, seventeen waltzers, countless merry-go-rounds (where live horses, giant chickens, and fat jumping frogs leapt off the ride with a rider on its back and bounded around the fairground), hundreds of toffee apple and candy floss stalls, twenty shooting galleries, corkscrews, ghost trains, rollercoasters (six), and much, much more.

Circling lower now she heard loud music, and multicoloured banners, flags, and pulsating lights came sharply into view.

They slowly dropped and landed just outside the fairground.

'Roll up! Roll Up! One and all - welcome to Franz Frenzy's Fantastic Fairy Fairground Extravaganza ... and, not forgetting, his Chillerific Big Top Circus!' the booming announcement echoed.

After Perigold had transformed back into his human-self, they walked along a muddy track with the thronging crowd which led to the box-office. Jesse saw all manner of excited fairy folk. Clearly, the fairground and circus was a magnetic attraction. There were not only the tiny and winged fairies, but creatures of colossal size.

Jesse was queuing up with hairless giants and freckled banshees, wart-ridden witches and pasty old warlocks, chubby ogres and ugly trolls, childsize gnomes and diminutive brownies. There were cheeky hunky punks who every now and again licked the ear of the fairy closest to them; clever-looking corrigans with their peculiar noses tucked in intellectual books, and fifty ghoulish spriggans, who kept nudging each other and pointing rudely at Jesse and her friends as if they recognised them.

'What an amazing place, stuck out here in the middle of nowhere,' Jesse said. 'Where have all these people come from?'

'All over the Kingdom of Finnigull and beyond,' Perigold said. 'Franz Frenzy's Attractions are legendary. He's been coming to this same spot for over a hundred years. He stays here for two weeks, and then moves on to another location. Alisbad is next, I believe.'

'How can this fairground help us find Jake Briggs?' Jesse wanted to know, suddenly shaking herself out of the illusion around her. 'Does someone here have information that might help us?'

'Er … something to help, yes,' Perigold said pensively. 'But more than this I cannot say.'

'Why not?'

'Please, don't push, Jesse. Trust me. By the time we leave this place, all will be clear.'

'This sounds very mysterious. I don't think I like it.'

'She should know a little of what's expected,' the Dragon Hunter said. 'You did when you took the shape-shifting chall-'

'Very well,' Perigold said. He shot the Dragon Hunter a sideways glance that was very cross. 'It seems I've been put in a difficult position.'

Jesse looked at them both nonplussed.

'I know your mother frowns on many of the

traditions of the Fairy Kingdoms,' Perigold went on, 'but this is one that she herself rose admirable to when she was your age. You see, not only is Franz Frenzy's attractions a magnet for fairground lovers all over the Fairy Kingdoms, but he is also the premier host to the Notorious Novice Shape-Shifting Challenge.'

'Sounds painful,' Jesse said, winking at Iggywig.

'Tis very painful,' Iggywig replied. 'Tis a fine sight me be a-seeing three years since. The winner be a-taking-'

'It's not about winning or losing,' Perigold cut in. 'The de Lacjard family has had its fair share of winners and losers over the centuries. Jesse will do her best, won't you?'

'Will I?' She was struggling to haul herself out of the shockwave. She had never considered herself a competitor, let alone a shape-shifter, although the idea of transforming into wondrous creatures appealed to her imagination no end.

'Of course. It's what your mother would want.'

'Maybe, but she's not here,' Jesse said. 'What - exactly - does this Notorious Novice Shape-Shifting Challenge expect from the competitors?'

'Ah - that's the problem, the reason I was not too keen to tell you too much. You see, no-one knows. Every year the Challenge is different.

It's the only way cheating can be minimised. But one thing is certain ...'

'What's that?'

'You'll be able to shape-shift with the best of us after the Challenge is over. Of that, I *am* certain. And without that skill, your search for Jake Briggs must end.'

'Why?'

'Because I know exactly where he is, and to rescue him will require far greater skill than it took to rescue your mother from Dendrith's Castle. Without shape-shifting, the rescue is impossible. So, you see, dear child, it's up to you to do your very best in the Challenge. Your own life and your friend's will depend upon it.'

'And the prize money?' the Dragon Hunter said. 'She has a right to know why we need that so badly.'

'Hmmm ... you are right, Hunter,' Perigold said, nodding. 'She should know all of it, I suppose.'

'All of what?' Jesse asked, growing more suspicious by the second.

'Jake Briggs's kidnappers want a ransom - ten million Heckles, I believe. The prize money will go some way to paying for his release.'

'Some way?'

'Forget it, Jesse.'

'I won't forget it. How much are you putting towards the ransom, Perigold?' Jesse asked firmly.

'Everything he and I own,' the Dragon Hunter said. 'That's more than you should know.'

Jesse stood in line, lost in thought. A ransom for Jake Briggs? It just didn't make sense. How much ransom had Perigold and the Dragon Hunter put up? Everything they owned? That sounded like an awful lot. And what could the Challenge be? Who else would she be up against? She felt completely unprepared, and small-minded now that she had learned how much Perigold and the Dragon Hunter were giving up for Jake. After all, they didn't even know him. They were doing it for her - for Jesse.

A few minutes later, an old hag poked her green face out from the box-office. She leered at them, displaying mouldy brown fangs. 'Do yer wanna ticket, or not?' she snapped.

'Er ... yes, please,' Jesse said.

'That'll be a thousand Heckles, and twenty Shindishes - each!'

Jesse suddenly realised to her embarrassment that she didn't have any money - not a Shindish to her name. She turned to her friends, but Perigold was ahead of the game. He handed over the money to the old hag, who snatched the coins out of his hand and shoved him a few triangular Shindishes in change.

'You'll need a map, deary,' she said, waving

a green Gameboy-looking device in Jesse's face. She smiled at Perigold. 'Don't wanna lose the little sweetie, or do you?'

'How much?' Perigold asked, ignoring her question.

'A thousand Heckles.'

Perigold handed over the money and handed the mapping device to Jesse.

'Have a horrid time,' the hag cackled. 'Hurry along. Next! That'll be a thousand Heckles, and twenty Shindishes - each!'

As they entered the fairground, Jesse looked carefully at the mapping device. It was just a bit smaller than a Gameboy, but the same shape. In the middle it had a large, round, convex view screen. There were four directional buttons which guided the user around a miniature holographic version of the fairground either manually or automatically.

She pressed a round button that said: *Automatic Start*. A great drum-roll blasted out the mapping device, followed by a holographic face of Franz Frenzy, the owner of the fairground and circus. He was a scrawny, tough-looking dwarf, with a long brown beard, and judging from the cracks and crevices that wrinkled his leathery brown face he must have been over two hundred years old.

'Thank you for purchasing a ticket for my Fantastic Fairy Fairground Extravaganza,' he said in an accent that sounded German to Jesse's ears, 'and, not forgetting, the Chillerific Big Top Circus! And a whopping thank you for buying a *Find-Your-Way* mapping device from one of our lovely box-office assistance. I know this device will become an invaluable friend as you're tickled, thrilled, chilled, shocked, rocked, rolled, horrified, petrified, and ... electrified by my fairground attractions.

'So, without any more preambles from Franz, hold tight and get ready for your hair to turn grey and rise in fright! Remember: the louder you scream, the faster you go!'

The fairground was a fantastic place, as Franz Frenzy had claimed - fantastic and rather scary. She visited a shooting gallery and Iggywig won her a fluffy bunny. She rode on the waltzers next, and staggered off, feeling as sick as a pig. Then she paused at Mystic Mo's Fortune Telling Booth and read the notices:

Have your fortune told by living tea leaves.
See your future in the crusty crystal ball -
And be amazed by the wonders that lie ahead.
Will you be rich and famous?
Will you live to be a thousand years old?
Mystic Mo is the Fortune Teller who knows.
What your future holds before it happens!
So give her a go! Two thousand Heckles!
A real bargain! Can you afford not to know?

'Tis a wise one be that Mystic Mo,' Iggywig said, nodding. 'All the Big Wigs and Bossy Folk be a-swearing by her. She be the best in the Kingdom.'

'Superstitious nonsense,' the Dragon Hunter scoffed.

'I'd like to know the future,' Jesse said. 'It sounds like fun.'

'The future cannot be known,' Perigold said seriously. 'Nothing is set in stone. We each make our own destiny.'

'Maybe,' Jesse said. 'But I still think it would be fun to hear what she has got to say. Her crusty crystal ball sounds like fantastic fun!'

'Waste of money,' the Dragon Hunter said. 'Why not have a ride on the Helter Skelter?'

'I'd rather see Mystic Mo.'

Mystic Mo's Fortune Telling Booth was exactly as Jesse had imagined. There was a small round table in the middle of the small square room. On the table she saw the crusty crystal ball, a pack of cards, a pot of steaming tea, two cups and saucers, and a bowl of sugar lumps. A smoky blue haze filled the room, which was lit by a single red candle placed next to the teapot.

On the tatty red walls, holographic faces winked and smiled, showing that they had once been satisfied customers of Mystic Mo's. There was even a gruesome holographic image of Dendrith, the witch, with the signed words, 'I was truly amazed by Mystic Mo's psychic powers.' Jesse spotted, too, the famous storyteller, Kayblade, and the Mayor of Alisbad. Judging by the happy grins they both had on their faces, they were very pleased with what Mystic Mo had predicted for their futures.

'One lump, or two, deary?' said the old, black-haired fortune teller, Mystic Mo. She was hunched over the table, pouring black tea into two, white, dinosaur bone cups. She was very tiny, a kind of shrunken figure, with puckered fingers and glowing black eyes.

Jesse did a double take because, moments before, Mystic Mo had not been sitting at the table; she'd just appeared out of thin air.

'I would have thought that you'd know how many sugar lumps she would take,' the Dragon Hunter said caustically. He had joined Jesse in the room, not wanting to leave her alone with a complete, and to his mind, mad stranger.

'There's much I know about this child's future,' Mystic Mo said. 'She is well-known in the Fairy Kingdoms. Her aura tells me that much.' She peered into the crusty crystal ball, while deftly dropping in two sugar lumps (exactly as Jesse would have done), stirring with a teaspoon, then handing Jesse the cup of tea. 'The crystal ball will tell me everything else there is to know.'

The Dragon Hunter made a scoffing sound through his nose, folded his arms, and tapped his foot impatiently on the floor.

'Please sit down, Jesse Jameson,' Mystic Mo said, smiling. 'Now if you cross my palm with two thousand Heckles, we can begin.'

'How do you know my name?' Jesse asked.

'She has heard us talking while we have been walking around the fairground,' the Dragon Hunter said. 'This is not fortune telling, but spying.'

'Your friend may well be a famous dragon slayer,' Mystic Mo said, still gazing misty-eyed into the crystal ball. 'But he has the manners of a pig eating its swill.'

Jesse stifled a giggle.

The Dragon Hunter's hand moved to the hilt of his sword. 'Insult me again, old hag,' he threatened, 'and I shall add your name to the long list of dragons I have killed.'

'Oh, please,' Jesse scolded. 'Stop the tough guy nonsense. Have you any idea how ridiculous you sound threatening Mystic Mo?'

The Dragon Hunter shuffled uneasily, and grunted something rude under his breath.

Jesse handed over the two thousand Heckles Iggywig had given her just before she entered Mystic Mo's booth, insisting she take it as a gift. Jesse had accepted it only as a loan which she intended to pay back the moment she was able.

'Now then, to answer your first question, Jesse Jameson,' Mystic Mo said, her eyes still fixed oddly on the crusty crystal ball. 'I saw your face and name in my crystal ball yesterday, so I knew that you would be coming soon.'

'But how does the crystal ball work?'

'If I told everyone the answer to that question, my dear, there would be no need for Mystic Mo, now would there?'

'I suppose not,' Jesse said. 'I was just interested, that's all.'

'I know, my dear. You have a keen mind, a questioning mind, and that's a good thing and a bad thing.'

Jesse waited for more, but something was happening to the crusty crystal ball. A white mist began to swirl inside it.

'I see ... I see ... I see ... great success, and awful betrayal, dear. There are too many faces, too many images to untangle. Ah, yes ... the mists become clear now. Someone you trust, someone very close to you, will betray you before this day is over. I am sorry to bring you this sad news. But all is not as it should be. There has been a terrible spell cast, a spell of terrible evil. Be very careful Jesse Jameson. Watch your back, my dear. Watch your back.'

Beware of the abyss with it's hidden stones.
Step on them in a figure of eight,
Otherwise you'll perish by the force of your own weight.
Reveal the steps you must take,
By tossing sand like fishing bait.

With this Mystic Mo snapped her eyes shut and said no more. A small blue elf hobbled into the room, appearing from behind a ruby red curtain at the far end.

'Mystic Mo says good-bye and good luck, and to be very afraid of the young witch Dendrith has sent to destroy you,' he said in a croaky voice. He handed Jesse the two thousand Heckles she had paid. 'No charge today. You know where the door is. You can see yourself out.'

Jesse got up from the table, wondering how Mystic Mo had communicated to the elf. As she left the old woman, who was still sitting motionless, eyes tightly shut in a trance state, Jesse wondered also who could possibly betray her? The Dragon Hunter? Perigold? Iggywig? It just didn't make any kind of sense. They were her friends. They had been through so much together. And who was the witch Dendrith had sent to destroy her?

Suddenly, stepping out into the hullabaloo of the fairground again, Jesse felt very afraid, even though she was surrounded by her friends. She found it hard to look them straight in the eye. Would one of them betray her before the end of the day?

Seven

The Shape-Shifting Challenge

'Will all novices for the Shape-Shifting Challenge please report to the House of Fun. Thank you. Have a horrid day!'

It suddenly dawned on Jesse that she had no idea *how* to shape-shift. She'd seen Perigold and her mother shape-shift, and wondered how they managed to do it with such apparent ease. But now, when the moment of truth had arrived, well ... she was ... clueless.

'Tis a-time to be a-hurrying to the Fun House,' Iggywig said.

'I know,' Jesse said. 'I ... er ...'

Perigold stepped in: 'I once told you, in the Knoll of Knowing, I believe, that shape-shifting was possible with training. Well, my dear child, today you will get the best training any shape-shifter can get.'

'But I-I-I don't know *how* to shape-shift.'

Perigold laughed. 'It's in your blood, Jesse. It's not so much how, but when. When to use it, yes, now that's vital. But to alleviate your concerns - this is a piece of advice I was taught a long time ago. First, *think* your shape; next - *see* your shape in your mind's eye; then - *say* your shape in your head - never out loud, otherwise an enemy may get an advantage. And finally you will *be* the shape. Don't fight the changes that will happen to your body. Welcome them - shape-shifting is a wonderful gift!'

'But I've never ever practised,' Jesse said, still feeling tense. 'What if I can't transform?'

'It'll be all right. Now go - you don't want the other Challengers to start without you.'

'Good luck,' the Dragon Hunter said. 'I will carry you shoulder high for the whole world to see after you win.'

'I'll try my best.'

'I know you will.'

'Tis a good luckings Iggywig be a-wishing on

Jesse Jameson,' the Gobbit said, smiling.

Jesse gave him a big hug and thanked him for his support.

'Take this, a little gifting that be a-coming in handy in a tricky situation.'

Iggywig handed Jesse a small rubber ball. 'Maybe Iggywig's gift be a-giving Jesse a little more luck, eh?'

'What's it called?'

'A Homingball Charm.'

'What do I do with it?'

'Throw it at your enemy ...'

'AND RUN LIKE THE CLAPPERS!' they laughed in unison.

She put the ball in her pocket and rubbed her sweaty hands nervously on her Forever Fitting Jeans. Using the *Find-Your Way* mapping device, she headed for the House of Fun, with Perigold, the Dragon Hunter, and Iggywig in tow.

The crowd gathered outside the House of Fun was enormous. Jesse nudged her way through to the stage where the flamboyant figure of Franz Frenzy stood, clutching a cordless microphone.

'One-two ... one-two ... testing ... testing,' he bawled, banging the mouthpiece.

'Get on wiv it, Frenzy!' a gang of drunken elves yelled, sloshing goblets of mead everywhere but in their mouths. 'Wot's this year's

Challenge?'

The crowd cheered, echoing the elves eagerness to know the nature of the Challenge. Jesse surged forward, and was almost crushed as she scrambled onto the stage. The crowd let out a massive roar, and applauded.

'At last, ladies and gentlemen,' Franz Frenzy said, raising his hand in Jesse's direction. His left eye twitched madly, like a roller-blind being pulled up and down at great speed. 'Our last, but by no means least, (we sincerely hope) shape-shifting challenger, Miss ... er ...' He beckoned Jesse over. 'What's your name, sweetie pie?'

She gave him an icy stare. 'Not miss, and not sweetie pie, just Jesse.'

Franz Frenzy smiled a big false smile, his left eye twitching; he ignored Jesse's retort. 'Family name?' he asked, a hard edge to his voice.

Jesse looked down at Perigold, the Dragon Hunter, and Iggywig. They were applauding wildly with the rest of the crowd.

'Jesse de Lacjard,' she said, and she could have sworn she saw Perigold wiping away tears from his eyes as she spoke.

'Jesse de Lacjard!' Franz Frenzy yelled. 'Give her a great big warm welcome. It's cold, and it's spooky, and it's ... right behind me - this year's Challenge, folks, is located in my very own ...

House ... of ... Fuuuuunnn!'

The crowd's roar almost deafened Jesse it was so loud.

'So, let's meet the other challengers before they embark on the Notorious Novice Shape-Shifting Challenge. All the way from the north of the Kingdom of Finnigull, representing the Castle Dendrith, Jagdrith, a trainee witch under the watchful and most evil eye of Dendrith herself.'

Most of the crowd booed and hurled dead frogs and toads and bats at the young witch. Jagdrith gathered them up and threw them back.

Jesse gulped. So Mystic Mo was right, she thought. This is not good, not good at all.

Jagdrith glided across the stage to Jesse and glared at her. Unusually for a witch, she had long blonde hair, and a pretty face, except for one repugnant feature: a monstrous hairy wart on the point of her chin that resembled a volcano about to erupt with adolescent puss.

'You don't fool me, Jameson,' she said acidly. 'Jesse de Lacjard my foot. You'll be as dead as my aunt - Gwendrith - by the time I've finished with you.'

Dead? Jesse thought, horrified. Gwendrith?

She shot a glance of undiluted hatred at Iggywig. 'And your sidekick, the Gobbit, will die a slow death, just like Gwendrith, in a Bubble

Charm, along with the rest of your pathetic guardians.'

Of course, Jesse thought. Iggywig had imprisoned Gwendrith in a Bubble Charm so that he could rescue her from a block of ice. What a horrible way to die, she thought.

Before she retreated back to her place, Jagdrith nodded to a dark figure standing at the front right of the crowd.

'And if you manage somehow to escape me, then an old friend of yours will do the honours later.'

Jesse sucked in a short breath, wincing from the grotesque sight of Kildrith's face. He sneered at her, showing a filthy black worm of a tongue.

'All the way from a hole in the ground on the banks of the River Blackwater, give it up for - Bragga Huggaton!' Franz Frenzy announced, his left eye twitching frantically.

The spotty-faced troll was massive, weighing in at least thirty stone. He was more than six feet tall, about half the size of the average adult troll. He wore a dirty food-stained orange tunic, which had a live snake tied around his ample waist as a belt. Hanging from the snakebelt by strips of leather were old chewed bones and a collection of razor-sharp knives. His skin was covered in green-scaled armour, which in the long distant past of Troll History would have grown inwards at the slightest hint of daylight, turning him into stone. But this had not happened now for almost a century, since the famous Charm Weaver and completely barking mad dwarf scientist, Doctor Dadilius Divine, injected some DNA from a light-loving tree slug, by the name of Edgar Alum Pie. Result: a Fairy Kingdom free of stone trolls!

'Arrraaghh!' Bragga Huggaton roared, clenching his football-sized fists, and shaking them in the air at the crowd as if he'd just scored the winning goal in an FA Cup Final. 'Arrrraaagghhh!'

Jesse could tell that he was not the brightest creature ever to be born in the Fairy Kingdoms. Recalling a few facts from the book *Fairy Tales, Legends and Myths* by Professor I. Kantellium, she knew that trolls struggled to complete whole sentences. Like great babies, they tended to point and yell, grunt and bawl to get what they wanted. They were also, she recalled with growing terror, ferocious flesh eaters, who weren't too fussy where they got their next meal. Bragga Huggaton looked extremely hungry, she thought.

'Let the Challenge begin!' Franz Frenzy announced, and the revolving doors of the House of Fun began to spin. 'Challengers, you have seven minutes to complete the challenge. May the beast fairy win!'

'Don't you mean *best* fairy?' Jesse said.

'I know what I said, and I know what I mean!'

'What is the challenge?' Jesse wanted to know, feeling a little more concerned by Frenzy's twitching eye.

'The Black Box will tell you. Use your *Find-Your-Way* to find the Black Box.'

'But-'

A loud shot from a starting pistol rang in

Jesse's ears, and Jagdrith, and Bragga Huggaton raced to get through the revolving doors first. Jesse sprinted close behind them narrowly slipping into the cubicle behind Huggaton. Jagdrith was like lightning, a good ten yards ahead of them.

Inside the House of Fun, Jesse stopped dead in her tracks. Now this was totally bizarre. The inside was like a giant warehouse. There were pulleys and grey metal escalators everywhere. Instead of rising at a forty-five degree angle like the ones she had ridden up and down on in the London Underground, or John Lewis's department store, these escalators were horizontal. There must have been twenty or more, with an eight foot gap between each level.

Jesse looked quickly around and spotted a small Black Box to her right. She couldn't believe her luck. She ran to it before the others noticed, and wrenched open the lid. Inside the box was a leather pouch. She picked it up. It was heavy. Opening it she could hardly believe her eyes, for inside was a large gleaming diamond.

'I am your prize,' the diamond said without any sign of a mouth. 'Collect three in total and you win the Challenge.'

She tied the string of the pouch through a belt loop of her jeans, making sure the opening was secured tightly.

Then, to her further amazement, fluorescence green holographic letters poured out of the box and letter by letter began to form words and sentences that hovered in the air. Jesse thought that Bragga Huggaton was on a hiding to nothing - he'd never be able to read an instruction.

Get to the top of this House of Fun
But don't you stop or down you'll come!
Another box is there waiting for you
Kick it open and then dive through!

Jesse hurried to the lowest escalator and hauled herself up. At the far end she could see a ladder that would take her to the next level, but she would have to run against the escalator's motion to get to it.

Jagdrith had found another Black Box and was now racing to the first escalator, transforming into ... a ... leaping sabre tooth tiger, who powered passed Jesse in one great bounding movement. Below, Bragga Huggaton scratched his big head stupidly, gazing around, not sure what to do next.

Jesse was unaware of the hundreds of cameras inside the House of Fun that filmed the Challengers' every move. She knew that to have any chance of catching Jagdrith she would have to shape-shift. But into what?

It came to her like a bolt from the blue.

JESSE JAMESON AND the bogie beast

... think your shape; next - see your shape in your mind's eye; then - say your shape in your head - never out loud, otherwise an enemy may get an advantage.

Yes! She had been this creature before - rescuing her mother from Dendrith and her evil Surgeons. But she'd had help from Iggywig, hadn't she? A Changing Charm, he'd called it. And there had been terrible side-effects; hideous beasts and horrendous pain!

... and finally you will be the shape. Don't fight the changes that will happen to your body.

Perigold's words swam round in her head. I can do it, she thought, with growing confidence. I have to do it! Now!

She thought of a bird - a swift - fast and light. She saw the swift clearly in her mind's eye. She said the word over and over again in her head. And then, with the most amazing explosion of noise and light and smells and sensations she had ever experienced before - BANG! The transformation happened in a flash.

Flying like the wind, Jesse sped higher and higher, beyond levels two, three, and four; up and up passed levels nine, ten, and eleven, and with a gleeful whistle she coasted by Jagdrith, who let out a fearsome roar at the sight of the tiny bird ahead of her, and tried to swipe her with her paw.

'Aarrrgggghhh!' yelled Bragga Huggaton as

he transformed into the most incredible sight Jesse had ever seen. 'Aaarrrggghhh!'

The gigantic oak tree rose from its roots at a tremendous speed. Its branches smashed all the escalators it bulldozed passed, sending shards of metal and bolts and nuts everywhere. Jagdrith was knocked from level sixteen by an outstretched branch, and as she tumbled head over paws she transformed into a bald eagle.

Jesse knew she had to reach the Black Box before the eagle devoured her. But the oak tree was crashing through level after level at a phenomenal rate.

Outside, the crowd roared and applauded the challengers' efforts. They gasped in horror, oohhed in delight; aaahhed in consolation at each twist and turn. Watching the contest from a wide screen next to the House of Fun, Perigold, the Dragon Hunter and Iggywig bit their lips, clenched their fists, and blew out hot air as the tension became unbearable.

Franz Frenzy was at the microphone, his frantic commentary spilling out around the fairground, where thousands had stopped to view the spectacle on enormous TV screens that were dotted around.

'Ah, yes - what a lovely mover young Jagdrith is - just look at that eagle ... that is shape-shifting at its best, folks - and what about our friend, Bragga? He might not be the brightest bulb in the show, but, boy oh boy, just look at that tree grow! And little Jesse, sweetie pie, how about that? I don't believe it - against all the odds - she's made it to the Black Bo- OUCH - I wouldn't want to be a feather in her wing - that branch must have stung - but what's this? Jagdrith is pulling a flanker all right - trust a witch to come good when it really matters - a ball of fire! Now that has got to hurt Huggaton! Call out the fire brigade someone - the tree is on fire! Get out the chestnuts! Toast your crumpets! Bragga is going up in smoke!'

The crowd cheered wildly, except the mead-swilling gang of drunken elves who booed and threw goblets at the screen.

Jesse and Jagdrith yanked open the Black Box together, and dived into the dark hole. It was completely mad, Jesse thought, as she tumbled down into the blackness. She caught a brief glimpse of Jagdrith's beak and talons, but something else was happening.

Jagdrith cackled loudly as she cast the spell, sending torrents of flames and sparks flying from the wand she was now waving as she transformed into her witch self.

The cascade of magic hit Jesse full in the chest, knocking her to the ground. She tried desperately to transform into something big enough to fight off the force of the spell, but she was confused. What had Perigold advised when shape-shifting? Think the shape? Then ... what else came next? She couldn't think, and something else was happening ...

It felt as if she were being inhaled through a giant straw. She was travelling very fast. The howling in her ears was thunderous. She tried to keep her eyes open but the whirl of green and red made her feel like vomiting. Then something sharp pricked the back of her neck, and she had a stupid thought: that was a needle. I'm being drugged so that I can't win the Challenge ... now spinning and twirling ... blinking through her eyes she saw a pulsating vision of witches and snatched fragments of the glitter and dazzle of the fireworks beyond. Where was she going?

She shut tight her eyes once more, praying it would cease, and then - she tumbled head first onto a wood and metal floor and felt the *Find-Your Way* mapping device shatter.

Giddy and battered, splattered in cobwebs, she got cautiously to her feet. She tapped the broken mapping device in her hand - nothing, not even Franz Frenzy's over the top presentation. She tossed the useless device away.

She was clearly not alone, for all around her in the dark recesses were ghosts and ghouls and skeletons. Grotesque-looking masks glared wide-eyed, snarling, looming down on her. Wriggling giant spiders dangled from thick strands of web.

This was a ghost train! But no ordinary ghost train - the terrifying inhabitants were not animated toys, but real and alive and howling and screaming at her. Suddenly, she realised she was standing on the railway track, and hidden from view for the moment, but closing with every breath, was a train hurtling towards her.

She tried to move off the track, but something snagged her foot. She glanced down to see that her ankle was trapped under part of the track.

Any moment now ... and the train would rush around the corner. Then, out the corner of her eye, she saw it: another Black Box. It was tucked in a darkened alcove, just two sides showing.

The train hurtled around the bend, its blinding light like a single giant eye. The track rumbled and shook, but still she couldn't free her foot.

She had to get to the Black Box first.

It was so close.

But the train was almost on top of her, its whistle blowing madly like a demented ghoul. And then the front of the train began to transform and melt, revealing an oversized cackling head - it was Kildrith!

Kildrith was the train!

Jesse's mind was ablaze with fear. In one

magnificent move, she *thought, saw,* and *said* in a split second. Her transformation buckled the track beneath her clawed foot and the careering train whizzed passed her, crashing through the wall. Bricks and mortar rained down on the dragon Jesse had become. She didn't feel a thing because of the iron armour of her scales. She felt stronger now than she had ever done. Her teeth and claws were like javelins and rapiers, and her swishing tail could crush an army.

She moved stealthily to the Black Box and with a flick of her claw the lid was flung wide. A jumble of letters flew out and formed five sentences in mid-air that glowed green in the gloom.

Whatever you do
Smash it hard
But you'd better be quick
Or else you're barred!
(Or worse, still, your jam could be jarred).

'Thanks for that,' said a tiny voice, and Jesse saw a blur of black and yellow dive into the box. A couple of moments later, a giant wasp buzzed out and in its mandibles it carried the second diamond.

Jesse lunged out; trying to swat the wasp, but it was too fast. She meant to shoot out a sizzling blast of fire to cook the wasp in mid-flight, but somewhere in her shape-shifting process something had gone drastically wrong. Instead of fire, she shot out a jet of water, which Jagdrith simply shook off. Before Jesse could transform into a creature more suited to give chase, Jagdrith flew speedily away into the darkness of the tunnel, muffled cackles echoing in her ears.

Jesse was livid. Jagdrith had stolen the second diamond and with it the chance to be one step closer to winning the challenge.

Transforming into a hummingbird, Jesse pursued her prey, determined now more than ever to claim the winning diamonds. Jake Briggs's release depended upon it.

When Jesse entered the Hall of Mirrors, her first thought was to transform back into herself. For the sight of a small colourful hummingbird, darting to and fro was most disconcerting. However, she resisted the urge to transform, continuing to search for Jagdrith and another Black Box. Anyway, she could think of no faster creature to change into.

The mirrors were all shapes and sizes, convex and concave, reflecting grotesque and distorted images. Inside the mirrors a strange energy brewed - taut threads of light erupting brightly, and then dimmed, then growing bright again as lightning flashed *inside* the mirrors. A bone-shaking crash of thunder swiftly followed,

and then more lightning which made the edges
of the mirrors look like spitting electrical cable,
white-hot with sparking current.

This was like no fairground Jesse had ever
visited before. Its very strangeness tingled her
spine with apprehension of what might happen
next.

'Aaarrgghhh!'

Bragga Huggaton crashed through one of
the mirrors to her right. At first Jesse assumed
that he was trying to smash her with the
enormous club in his left hand, but then she
saw Jagdrith's wasp, dive-bombing the troll. She
flew in and out, stinging his fat, flat nose.

'Aaaarrggghhhh!' he yelled, swiping his club
at her again.

CRASH!

Another mirror shattered into small slithers
of glass, unleashing a storm of hail, lightning
and deafening thunder. Jesse felt incredibly
vulnerable now, as she dodged hail stones that
as a hummingbird could do her a great deal of
damage.

What shape next? she wondered.

Then-

It suddenly dawned on Jesse that Huggaton
didn't have a club in his hand; his hand *was* the
club, a partial transformation she had not seen
before. At about the same time as that particular
revelation, she had another - glancing up, about

ten feet off the ground and hovering of its own accord, she spotted a Black Box. But there was one problem: was it a real Black Box, or merely a reflection from the thousands of mirrors in the hall?

Jesse knew she needed to stab at the box to check it. She needed to act fast. So she transformed her body and head into a sleek white horse, her legs into an antelope's legs, and her tail into a lion's tail. The single horn which grew from her head had a base of pure white, a middle of gold and black, and a sharp tip of vivid crimson.

The unicorn leapt at the Black Box, thrusting its horn at the base. Glass rained down as the mirror smashed, covering her with razor-sharp shards. She didn't notice the blood trickling from her wounds, as she leapt at the next box, but the outcome was the same.

CRASH!

Huggaton smashed another mirror, unleashing another wild thunder and hail storm. Lightning singed Jesse's tail, skimming from mirror to mirror before exploding through the ceiling. Plasterboard and dust covered them like flour from a sieve. Huggaton sneezed and the force of the blast knocked Jagdrith's wasp to the ground. Stunned, and covered in green snot, Jagdrith span helplessly in a circle, one of her wings torn.

Huggaton seized his chance and stamped hard on the dazed wasp, twisting and grinding his heel around, until a diamond slid out from under his boot like a slippery chunk of ice.

Box or diamond? Jesse thought, feeling woozy and light-headed from all the shape-shifting. Her mind was in a spin. She had to think and act quickly. What to do?

Suddenly, emerging from beneath Huggaton's boot, and winding around his calf and now up his thigh, Jagdrith had transformed into a python. The snake was absolutely enormous, crushing the troll's leg so that he collapsed to the ground, writhing in pain.

'Aaarrrggghh!'

Jesse galloped to the diamond and grabbed it in her mouth. Transforming with speed and growing skill, (and despite the raging headache that throbbed in her temples) she changed into herself, bagged the diamond, and then dived at one of the Black Boxes above her. Before she hit it with a thud, she transformed into a sledgehammer. The box exploded into hundreds of pieces, and the third winning diamond arched high in the air, then tumbled as if in slow motion ... towards ... her transforming open hand.

'Got it!' she cried, catching the diamond in her palm.

'That's mine!' Jagdrith hissed, transforming

into her witch self but for a hideous snake's head. She snatched the diamond from Jesse's grasp; Jesse wrestled it back again, but lost it.

Huggaton jumped to his feet, veins throbbing in his temples, veins standing out from the sides of his thick neck like bloody ropes. Although he was wheezing like a winded elephant, he managed to knock the diamond from Jagdrith's hand, as he collapsed in a heap from Jesse's sledgehammer blow to his solar plexus. He keeled over, holding his fat belly, crying for his mummy.

But it was not over yet.

Descending around them, blocking all routes of escape, heavy iron gates slammed down. Above them, a glass vacuum the size of the entire Hall of Mirrors slowly expelled the air, pressing down on them like a massive plunger inside a syringe.

Whatever you do
Smash it hard
But you'd better be quick
Or else you're barred!
(Or worse, still, your jam could be jarred).

Bagging the third winning diamond, Jesse tried to unravel the clue that the previous box had spewed out, but there was so much to smash in the Hall of Mirrors, she didn't know where to begin. The bars had certainly come down, and above her the glass vacuum looked very much like a giant jam jar. Each breath of air became harder to inhale, as the plunger dropped faster now. She felt dizzy, and gasped ... wheezed ... choking ... unable to draw in enough breath to fill her lungs.

In desperation she threw the pouch of diamonds against one of the few remaining mirrors, watching it shatter. Her world faded quickly, and a deep cold darkness replaced her struggling for breath.

Unconsciousness.

A vision - the Bogie Beast, a crow, strange haunting fiddle music, a city beneath the earth, beautiful and peaceful, a ruby red sunrise, dragons gliding gracefully through the still cool air, children riding them with skill and-

Iggywig's comical face swam into Jesse's view. It was swiftly followed by Perigold, and a concerned Dragon Hunter. They were all kneeling around her; she lying comfortably on cushions spread out on the stage.

'She's awake,' Franz Frenzy announced to the crowd.

A massive cheered echoed around the fairground.

'Our winner is awake!'

More cheering was preceded by a stupendous fireworks display, and the prize-giving, which Jesse managed from a wooden chair brought onto the stage by a hunky punk. The large piece of white parchment Franz Frenzy awarded to Jesse read:

For Winning the Notorious Novice
Shape-Shifting Challenge of Finnigull,
I, Franz Frenzy, hereby honour the grand
sum of-

'Let him through,' someone said.

'Yeah, make way over there.'

'He looks like he's seen a Spriggan!'

Jesse's celebrations were short-lived. Just then an exhausted dwarf ran on to the stage, grabbing the microphone out of Franz Frenzy's hand.

'I've ... I've ... I've just come from Alisbad. It's ... it's awful, I tell you. Really bad. One minute it was there, the next - nothing. Wiped clean. The landscape, the buildings, the people, everything gone! Loath Town is gone, too, and Dendrith's Castle, and the Frozen Forest.' He shook his head, the deadly silent crowd clinging to his every word. 'And it's headed this way! Run for your lives! If you value your life - run for it ... NOW! The Rumble is coming! Do you hear me? THE RUMBLE IS COMING!'

Eight

Shimmering City of Slime

Jesse heard the Rumble a good five minutes before the dust storm heralded the cracking of the earth. Its tone was so deep that it shook tree roots loose from the ground and reduced buildings to rubble in seconds. It was millions of times more powerful than all the earthquakes that there had ever been. Its roar was so loud that no voice, no matter how it screamed, could be heard.

But that was not the worst of it.

The Rumble fed on the people's discontent, the way a hungry lion feeds on its prey. Everyone who had felt calm and contented with their lot in life suddenly felt discontented and had a thirst for change that just had to be quenched. Everyone, that was, who managed to survive the total annihilation that came in the Rumble's wake. Only those who had the ability to take to the sky survived. No-one else stood a chance. The Rumble wiped the landscape clean like a blackboard eraser wiping chalk, leaving darkness - an empty void of nothingness where life had once been.

Jesse and Perigold transformed moments before the Rumble hit Franz Frenzy's Fantastic Fairy Fairground Extravaganza and his Chillerific Big Top Circus. High above the Ferris Wheels, they watched in horror, with Iggywig perched high on the ridged back of Jesse's dragon and the Dragon Hunter sitting astride Perigold's flying horse. The Rumble swallowed whole the Big Top, the Waltzers, the Dodgem Cars, the Whirling Wheezers and the Helter Skelter. Next it devoured the Merry-go-rounds, Rollercoasters, stalls of rock, nougat, fudge, toffee apples, and candy floss. Thousands of witches, warlocks, and flying beasts took to the air in a great dark cloud of fluttering cloaks and smoking broomsticks. Thousands more creatures without the skill of flight tried to out run the Rumble, or simply dropped to their knees and prayed to whatever god or deity they thought might save them. All of them vanished without trace, along with the Standing Stones, Hemlock Hill, and the goblin mines to the north.

'I don't believe my eyes,' Jesse shouted, but no-one heard her because the clamour was overpowering. She stared into the nothingness, jaw dropped open like a fish out of water.

The further they flew over the Mountains of Mourn, the greater the distance between them and the Rumble became. Fifteen minutes later, the noise had subsided enough for them to hear each other when they spoke, but the weather was turning bitterly cold. Great clouds of billowing breath poured from them as they spoke.

'Where are we going?' Jesse asked, finding it easier than she had expected to talk through a dragon's mouth, although she found it hard to pronounce the "th" sound without letting out a blast of fire.

'There is a dormant volcano that myth and legend claims is a secret entrance into the mountain,' Perigold explained.

'How can it be a secret if you know about it?' Jesse said sceptically.

'It is not a very well kept secret,' Perigold admitted. 'But not many people know about it.'

'Tis a dark secret that my people be a-knowing very well,' Iggywig said, making Jesse giggle. 'Tis a bad place, a city of evil doings beneath the Mountains of Mourn. Be a-causing Iggywig great fearings in my tummy.'

'Some secret,' Jesse scoffed.

'But the kind soothsayer be a-right,' Iggywig said. 'Tis a secret where the entrance be. For no creature ever be a-leaving the City of Evil once they be a-finding it.'

'That is why its whereabouts remains a deadly secret,' Perigold said. 'No-one, as Iggywig rightly points out, has ever returned to the Upper Kingdoms to tell another.'

'Maybe they never got there,' Jesse said speculatively.

'Maybe they did,' the Dragon Hunter added, 'but they never got out alive to tell their tale?'

'Is this where you think Jake is being held?' Jesse breathed.

'I know it is,' Perigold said. 'It's where we have to take the ransom in exchange for your friend.'

Jesse shook her head. 'It still doesn't make any sense. Why on earth would anyone want to hold Jake Briggs for a ransom? He's a good friend, but he ... well ... he has no special gifts, or anything like that. He's just an ordinary boy.'

'You are wrong, Jesse,' Perigold said. 'Jake Briggs is the perfect hostage to hold up for a ransom.'

'How come?'

'His stories are invaluable, because of his close friendship with you. He can tell his captor so many things about you. Things which your father, the Bogie Beast, has missed not being around while you have grown up with humans. You are the child he cherishes the most above all of his many children. He is obsessed with you being by his side, father and daughter reunited.'

'But he's not my father,' Jesse said. 'I don't know him. He's a frightening stranger, a beast of evil and wickedness.'

'True, but he *is* your father, all the same, however difficult that is for you to accept.'

'He's not a father to me,' Jesse said. 'Roger Jameson is my dad. He's the one who was there for me. He's the one who has loved me and looked after me - not the Bogie Beast!'

There was little more to be said on the matter. Jesse's anger was burning her cheeks - that much was clear. They flew further and further over the mountains, passing through swirling clouds. It was growing colder and colder, and soon they were dazzled by the slowly lowering sun ahead of them. Soon it would be dark.

Half an hour later, they spotted a beacon watchtower. Then snaking over the vast range of mountains they saw a wall, a great wall, guarded by thousands and thousands of creatures. From the safety of the height at which they now travelled, it was impossible to say exactly what breed of fairy manned the wall. But whoever they were it was guaranteed that they would be well-trained, obedient, and ruthless in their duty for their master, the Bogie Beast.

'I hope we don't have to meet them face to face,' Jesse said. 'I think we are slightly out-numbered.'

'Agreed. But we have to land,' Perigold said.

'Where?'

'Over there,' he said, motioning with his head. 'See it? The volcano entrance to the Bogie Beast's subterranean city.'

Jesse narrowed her eyes, squinting hard against the fading light of the setting sun. 'Yes,' she said, just making out the enormous black hole. 'I see it.'

As they slowly began to descend towards the rim of the volcano, Jesse's heart lurched. Her mind was flooded with dark dread. In her head, she heard over and over again the terrifying words of the vision that was about to come true: *soon, my child, we shall be together again ...*

Standing on the rim, they considered their next move. The mouth of the volcano was huge and dark, but a long way down they could make out tiny flashing lights.

'Is that the subterranean city?' Jesse asked.

'I think so,' Perigold said. 'Follow me down. Stay as close as possible.'

Jesse swooped down quickly, smelling the sulphurous stench of the volcano. Her dragon sense of smell was so acute that she could name any creature by the slightest whiff of a scent. Below them, she could smell elfins - lots of them.

As they flew deeper into the volcano, they could see that the flashing lights were just a few amongst millions of lights. The shimmering subterranean city before them was bigger than London, with tall glass buildings and brightly lit streets, teeming with creatures. Some walked, others flew, while many hovered on flyboards very similar to Iggywig's contraption. Jesse saw children everywhere, many flying on dragons or griffins, or giant birds that looked like pterodactyls.

Perigold led them to the roof of one of the tallest buildings, where a crowd of elfins were waiting for them below. In their hands, they carried strange devices - which seemed to be small towers of swirling light. Chained between two elfin guards, Jesse saw Jake Briggs. Her heart gave a small jump. He was alive!

Then came something she had not expected.

Just as they landed on the roof, elfin guards closing in on all sides, a strange shimmering force slithered across the rooftop. It was slushy like melting black ice. No, not ice, but a slimy black oil. It was about twenty yards in diameter. A raging invisible heat burned from it, making Jesse shield her face with her dragon's claws.

Jesse transformed into herself, so that Jake could see who she was. He still looked terrified.

'Jake!' she called out. 'It's me - Jesse Jameson!'

Jake's mouth dropped open in surprise, and he began to sway, in the middle of a faint.

'Jake! No!'

It was a typical response, she thought. Some things never change. He fell forwards.

Jesse set off at a run, the Dragon Hunter right behind her. But she was too late. Jake was slumped on the floor, unconscious, a trickle of blood running from a cut on the side of his face.

'We have the ransom,' Jesse said, slowing at the edge of the pool of black slime. She felt faint herself now that she was so close to the dark ooze. 'Hand over Jake and we'll be on our way.'

A figure gradually rose out of the slime, dripping blobs of sludgy blackness. Its heat seemed to penetrate Jesse's bones and lungs, making it hard for her to breathe or move. She was forced to squint her eyes because they stung so much. She shielded her face with burning hands, expecting the figure to reveal itself as her father, the Bogie Beast.

'I am the Negotiator, the Bogie Beast's

representative,' the figure said in a crackling voice, its features fluid and dark. Even though it opened a gaping hole in its head to speak, all Jesse could see was black sticky goo. 'It is not you I need to conclude the deal with. It is *her.*'

Jesse turned to see where the Negotiator's malformed dripping hand was pointing. She couldn't believe her stinging eyes. Perigold transformed into Dendrith, and the foul stinking witch howled madly and then chanted a charm:

Revenge is sweet, my revenge complete. Hubble, bubble, double, trouble. Imprison this creature in a deadly bubble.

A flash of red light tumbled out of her finger tips and Iggywig was knocked to the ground. When he got to his feet, he was locked inside a bubble that resembled the one in which he'd trapped Gwendrith. A red noxious gas slowly filled the bubble, and Iggywig began to cough and splutter. He was choking, being gassed to death.

Jesse's mind had gone vacant with shock. She stood there gazing at Iggywig, Jake, the Negotiator and Dendrith. Her eyes flitted from one to the other with a blooming horror. This was bad. Very bad. They had been trapped! Dendrith as Perigold? What had happened to Perigold? What had she done to him?

'Where is Perigold?' she shouted at the witch.

'Where is Perigold,' Dendrith echoed back in a mocking voice. She wafted her bony hand about like a mad conductor without an orchestra, flicking her hood down to reveal a mass of matted black hair, and a grotesque twisted grin. It was a face so loathsome and disgusting that Jesse's mind couldn't begin to understand it.

'Tell me where he is!'

'No.'

'TELL ME WHERE HE IS?'

'Guess, my pretty. If you dare.'

'What do you mean? What ... have ... you done to him?'

'No more than you did to my sister, Gwendrith!' the witch raged. 'Does that answer your question?'

'NO!' Jesse screamed. 'You wouldn't!'

Dendrith gave Jesse a black look, empty of all feeling, a void of hatred. 'I did. Perigold is dead.'

'How ... could ... you?' she sobbed.

'Easily,' the witch said. She clicked her fingers. 'As easily as that.'

'You are sick and evil,' Jesse mumbled, wiping tears from her eyes.

'Thank you, child, that's the kindest thing anyone has ever said to me.'

'Sick and mad.'

'Yes, I am, aren't I?'

JESSE JAMESON AND the bogie beast

'I hate you,' Jesse snarled.

'Good. I hoped you would.'

'Sick.'

Dendrith cackled madly, waving her hands about wildly, her tumbling long black hair fanned out behind her. 'You really are pathetic, my pretty,' she spat. 'Just look at you. A blubbering wreck. Pathetic. If it weren't for your father's great powers, and the fact that I'm at a disadvantage here in his shimmering city, I'd make you show me some long overdue respect-'

'How can anyone respect you?' Jesse sniped. 'You earn respect, not demand it with threats and bullying and selfishness!'

'My pretty,' she mocked. 'A temper! I like that. It feeds my soul. Your hatred feeds my hunger. What else can you conjure from your twisted opinions?'

'Twisted? Me? You are the twisted one!'

'If you could see yourself now, my pretty,' Dendrith taunted. 'Oh, if you could see yourself now. Your anger is beautiful to behold. Your rage is ... lovely!'

Jesse suddenly stopped herself. It was a rare moment of self-awareness, where she could watch her words and actions in a state of complete calm. The Rumble and Dendrith feed from the same trough, she thought. Be calm, and cool, and clear. Don't give in to her bitterness and warped sense of reality. Be still.

Let her evil thoughts go. You are so much more than she is.

'What's wrong, child? Choking on your own tongue?'

Jesse felt a surge of anger, but somehow managed to bottle it. Her mind was thinking about Perigold. Was he really dead? Murdered by Dendrith? It didn't bear thinking about.

'Oh, you are no fun, Jesse Jameson! I am disappointed.'

'My master thanks you, witch,' the Negotiator cut in. 'Now leave us, before he changes his mind. Take what is yours and leave his daughter be.'

Jesse heard the Negotiator's words, but did not respond to them. At that moment she was more concerned with the spluttering that was coming from inside the smoke-filled bubble. Suddenly, Iggywig's face and hands pressed against the skin of the bubble, gasping for breath. He was wide-eyed, and sucking hopelessly like a fish that had been laid on a river bank to die. What had she been thinking? How could she have wasted precious moments arguing with Dendrith?

Jesse twisted around to run towards Iggywig, a boiling panic erupting in her chest. For the first time in her life she lost all sense of self-preservation. She had to get to Iggywig and release him at all costs. Her friend was dying right before her eyes! But as she started forward, something grabbed her shoulders, and a burning heat seared through her. It was the Negotiator's clasping hands. The pain made her sink to her knees.

'No!' she managed to scream, as the Dragon Hunter unleashed his sword of light, bringing it down to within an inch of the Negotiator's throat. 'Run! Save yourself!'

Even as she spoke them, she knew that they were foolish words. The Dragon Hunter had never run from anything or anyone in his life. He was a warrior, her guardian.

'Let her go, or I will kill you,' the Dragon Hunter snarled. His golden eyes narrowed to slits, beams of light scanning the Negotiator for the slightest hint of movement. 'Do it now! Back away - slowly!'

The Negotiator reluctantly unravelled its slimy hands from her shoulders, and sank back into its pool of oozing darkness. Without a word, it slithered away, shrinking into a small puddle-sized blob, then smaller and smaller into a slither of goo.

CRACK!

It vanished, leaving a puff of black acrid smoke.

Jesse got gingerly to her feet, rolling her shoulders as if a great heavy weight had been lifted. She glanced across at Iggywig, but all she could see was the smoke inside the bubble. She feared the worst. He was surely dead, and the witch who had caused her so much suffering already was no longer opposite her.

Where had she gone?

Jesse wheeled around. The witch had seized her opportunity. Dendrith had Jake Briggs in her grasp, his arms and legs and head limp and dangling. He looked like a rag doll. And she was so much stronger than Jesse could ever have imagined.

'Let him be!' Jesse yelled, trying to will her legs to give chase, as they bent beneath her like rubber. The Negotiator had somehow drained her energy.

Dendrith glided across the rooftop with Jake in her arms as if she were carrying a small puppy. She rose vertically at a great speed, her cloak and hair billowing and fluttering like a giant bat. She was laughing insanely, drool leaking from her mouth, mumbling about the Golden Glow she was going to extract from Jake; ranting on about the look of total terror she had seen on Perigold's dying face, and how the revenge for her sister's death was now complete.

Jesse was too upset and weak to curse the witch again. She slid to the floor on her hands and knees. She really did feel very odd. Her strength and energy were ebbing away like water from a sieve. But who or what was draining them?

BANG!

A flash of purple light shattered the bubble, and stumbling from the clouds of red smoke Iggywig came into view. He collapsed just feet away from Jesse, coughing and spluttering. His face was blue, his eye bulging. It had been a close call, but he'd escaped - just - with his life.

The Dragon Hunter ran out of the smoke, and gathered up Jesse and Iggywig, one under each arm. 'We are in the open here, sitting ducks. We need to regroup, recover our energy.'

'What energy?' Jesse muttered, feeling tired and defeated. She could hear in the faint distance a haunting melody of fiddle music. It faded in and faded out. All around her was becoming a whirling blur ...

The Dragon Hunter hurtled passed the static elfins, who were continuing to point their strange pulsating devices at them. Jesse was expecting a volley of shots to ring out. But the elfins were not holding weapons. Not a single blast of light, or laser. Nothing. What were they carrying?

As the Dragon Hunter reached the edge of the roof, he could see below, a staircase winding down the side of the building. It was the only escape route.

'Put me down!' Jesse demanded. 'I've got to save Jake!'

'Tis a rescue we must be a-making,' the Gobitt spluttered, but it was clear that he was in no fit state to stand on his own two feet, let alone attempt to rescue Jake Briggs from the quickly escaping Dendrith.

'Not now,' the Dragon Hunter said. 'This is not a good time to stand and fight.'

'What?' Jesse said, amazed. Had she heard correctly? Surely the Dragon Hunter was not running away?

Jesse followed the Hunter's nodding head, and saw exactly why it was not a good time to fight: their father, the Bogie Beast was emerging from a pool of black slime just a few yards away. He was not alone. His army of darkness following him was vast, rising from tens of thousands of pools of slime on every rooftop she could see. They were surrounded. There was no way out.

'This looks bad,' Jesse said feebly, feeling light-headed and weak. Somewhere in the back of her mind she heard music - a single haunting fiddle.

The Dragon Hunter grunted, scanning for a bolt hole. 'If I thought I could kill him and get you out of here, I would not hesitate,' he said through gritted teeth.

It was the first time Jesse had heard the Dragon Hunter talk about their father, and she was not surprised that his hatred was equal to hers.

'What now?' Jesse asked, not able to fight the over-powering drowsiness that made it impossible for her to keep her eyelids open a moment longer.

'A good question,' the Dragon Hunter said. 'I'll let you know when I think of an answer.'

But Jesse didn't hear him. She was limp and unconscious in his arms.

Nine

Mind Control

From the depths of a dark place, where she could not move an inch or speak a word, Jesse heard them talking.

'Tis a Wide Awake Charm that be a-doing the trick.'

'Are you certain it will work?'

'Be a guaranteed to be a-working, kind slayer.'

'Who by?'

'Iggywig, of course.'

'How can you be so sure?'

'Be a-working for thousands of years for my people.'

'But will it work on Jesse?'

'Tis guaranteed.'

'Then you try it first.'

'Be not a wise thing to be a-doing, kind slayer.'

'Why?'

'Wide Awake Charm be a-sending those who are already awake fast a-sleepings.'

'How long for?'

'There be no telling, but some Gobbit folk be a-sleeping for weeks ... months ... even years.'

'You are a liar.'

'Kind slayer, Iggywig cannot be a-lying.'

'You also claim that you can't die, but I don't believe that either.'

'Death cannot be a-taking me, kind slayer. Tis true. I am a forever living - four thousand, two-hundred, and ten years.'

'You were almost dead when I rescued you from the Bubble Charm, so do not insult me by claiming that you cannot die.'

'But tis truth, kind slayer. Iggywig be like a caterpillar that forever be a-changing into a butterfly.'

'What do you mean?'

'Be a-striking Iggywig with your slaying sword.'

'Are you serious?'

'Yes, Iggywig be.'

'But I will kill you with one blow.'

'No, kind slayer, tis not a-possible. Iggywig will be a-changing, yes. One form be a-changing to another form. That is all.'

Jesse heard the Dragon Hunter unleash his sword of light from its scabbard. She tried to scream out: NO! But her lips were paralysed. She could not move a single muscle. In the darkness she laid there. She had no idea where she was; but somewhere close by she could hear sirens and shouting, orders being given, and she thought that the Bogie Beast's army was trying to find them. In amongst the racket she could hear the fiddle music again, getting stronger now.

'Are you ready, Gobbit?'

'Be as ready as a-ripe malgrim a-falling from a tree.'

'Then prepare to die.'

'Tis no preparation needed. Tis impossible for Iggywig to-

Jesse could only imagine the sharp thrusting pain of the white hot blade. She heard Iggywig squeal in anguish, and tried to get up. But she couldn't move. Not even a tear fell from her eye. Nothing but sound and darkness and the sensation of numbness where a body should have been.

'That is mightily impressive,' she heard the Dragon Hunter acclaim.

There was a sound like a muffled mini-explosion, a high-pitched whistle, the smell of burning flesh (yes, her sense of smell was working, too), and a deafening rustle of unfurling wings.

'That is most impressive, Gobbit. Truly you are what you say. I would not have believed it, if it were not for my own eyes. What a magnificent creature you have become through your survival of death.'

'Iggywig be a-thanking you, for your blow was the least painful death and rebirth me be a-having to endure for many a-century.'

'An honour, Gobbit. I have changed my opinion. Will you accept my apology for the insults I have spat at you?'

'Tis no problem. Iggywig be accepting your sorrying. Now shall we be a-giving the Wide Awake Charm to our good friend, Jesse?'

She heard Iggywig click his fingers twice, and then he mumbled some strange incantation in a lisping, lilting language that she guessed was Ancient Gobbit. 'Torrauglarantula -yak! Torra … ugla … rantula - yak!'

She heard the sound of sparks crackling, though saw no river of them leaving Iggywig's fingertips. Nothing. She was still stuck inside the darkness, unable to move. The fiddle music came again like a ghost - translucent and other worldly. She could smell a foul stench, like rotten cabbages and turnips, and there was the eerie sound of dripping water. She heard a scurrying somewhere in the distance, and the sound of clanking armour, followed by shouting.

'Search the sewer,' she heard a gruff voice yell.

'Yes, sir!'

More clanking of armour ...

'Let us hurry. The Bogie Beast's forces seem to be closing in.'

'Tis a-time to be a-running like the clappers, Iggywig be a-thinking.'

If she could, Jesse would have laughed. But there was a new sensation now, as if floating. What was going on?

'Are you strong enough to run, or shall I carry you under my arm, too?'

'Be a-feeling stronger than a Finnigullian firecracker, kind slayer. Iggywig's new form be a-created for the runnings and flyings.'

'Very well. Let us stay close. This sewer is no doubt full of dangerous creatures.'

Jesse smelled the terrible reek of the sewer as she was carried under the Dragon Hunter's arm. Although she couldn't see, she could imagine how dark and damp it might be. She heard them sloshing through filthy waist-high water, and the high-pitched squealing of creatures she thought might resemble rats.

'The Bogie Beast's soldiers are closing in fast. Take the next left. We will crawl along one of the narrow sewer inlets. They seem to lead upwards, maybe to a manhole cover and-

A blinding flash of light went off inside

Jesse's head. Then the grotesque features of her father appeared. No matter how hard she tried she couldn't shut him out. She could see a malformed shadow. He advanced slowly, wheezing with every icy breath. He extended his long, pale fingers and opened his luminous green slits of eyes.

'Daughter. So good to see you again. You seem to be slightly enfeebled. Let me help you.'

'Never!' Jesse shouted in her head. 'I never want your help! I'd rather die!'

'That may be your wish now, daughter, but you are confused. Once you know my side of the story, then maybe things between us will be as they should.'

'There is no side to your story. You were never there for me. You left me and my Mum to look after ourselves, and that ... is exactly what we did. Without you!'

'Is that what they told you?' He extended a slimy hand towards her face, but she recoiled away. 'How sad, that you know nothing of our time together when you were a small child.'

'You lie.'

'How sad that you know nothing of our time together as a family - just you, me, and your mother.'

'Liar!'

'How sad that your mother never told you that it was *she* who deserted me. It was *she* who sent me away, banished me from your life so that she could live amongst the humans as one of their kind with you all to herself. It was your mother who made those decisions, not me. All I ever wanted was to be with you, my daughter.'

'YOU ARE A LIAR!'

'Not me. I am your father. I couldn't lie to you. But they have. They have done a splendid job on you, Jesse. I have to congratulate them for the glamour they have thrown up around you all of these years. But all of that will change now that we are together again, here in my domain.'

'You are sick and evil and I want nothing to do with you!'

'Such a shame that you have been so blinded by the humans and the soothsayers I paid to care for you.'

'What do you mean - paid to care for me?'

'Oh, I see,' the Bogie Beast said forlornly. 'They didn't tell you.'

There was a vexatious look of victory about the Bogie Beast. He gloated in the deliberate silence.

'I should have known that the de Lacjards would try to poison your mind against me, steal you away - if they could. You see, your mother had help. You think that your mother and Perigold are your friends, but they are not. They have betrayed you ... poisoned your mind.'

'They haven't stolen me or poisoned my

mind against you. You abandoned me! I hate you without any help from them or anyone else!'

'I have to applaud them. They have done a convincing job on both you and my son, Richard, the Dragon Hunter. But once you have come to accept the truth, daughter-'

'I AM NOT YOUR DAUGHTER!'

'Of that, you seemed convinced, but you are my daughter. And you are precious to me. You will come to see this, and our love will grow.' He grimaced and a thick green slime oozed from the side of his disfigured mouth and ran down his chin. 'A father and daughter should be-'

'I AM NOT YOUR DAUGHTER!'

'I shall leave you to think over our little chat. You need time to come to terms with the truth.' He tried to smile, but all that surfaced was a wicked grin. 'Not long now, my child, before my followers bring you safely to me and then we shall be together again ...'

The Bogie Beast's face disappeared, and Jesse was left alone in her darkness, a head full of questions. Time together? All I ever wanted was to be with you? His side of the story? Blinded by the humans and the soothsayers he paid to care for me? Lies! All of it! Jesse thought. But the seeds of doubt had been planted. There were many questions she needed to ask Perigold and her mother, but that was not possible. She realised that without answers, her doubts would continue to grow. And that made her very scared indeed.

'Now Iggywig be a-stirring the potion thirteen times. There ... finished. Tis a magic that Iggywig be a-knowing will be a-working - a Sleep Walking Potion. Be a-keeping Jesse's mouth a-opening as wide as a-possible, kind slayer.'

'A Sleep *Walking* Potion?'

'Tis a powerful magic that not be a-using for many a century by my people.'

'Does it have any side effects?'

'One or two.'

'Go on.'

'Tis not one memory that Jesse will be a-remembering once the potion be a-wearing away.'

'Wearing off?'

'No, a-wearing away.'

'Wearing away what?'

'Jesse's rememberings. All of them be a gone.'

'I don't like the sound of this. How far back? Exactly?'

'From the moment she be a-swallowing the potion. That be all.'

'But she'll be able to walk and talk and act normally, yes?'

Iggywig scratched his head, and pulled a thoughtful face. 'Yes,' he said eventually, but he didn't sound convincing. 'I think so.'

'You think so?'

Iggywig nodded.

'But you are not sure?'

Iggywig shook his head. 'Be rare cases when Sleep Walking Potion be a-going a little mad.'

'What happens?'

'Tis nothing to be a-worrying about.'

'What happens?' the Dragon Hunter persisted.

'Sloshiness.'

'What's that?'

'Legs not be a-doing as they be a-tolding. Funny walk be a-coming and a-going when you be a-least expecting.'

'Will this sloshiness slow us down?'

'No!' Iggywig said, laughing. 'Be a-speeding Jesse up so fast that we be a-struggling to keep up!'

They had stopped, that much Jesse could tell. The floating sensation had ceased, and although she couldn't feel her mouth, she could smell the gross potion that Iggywig had somehow concocted. She was glad that she couldn't taste it, and had no idea whether or not she had taken it until a remarkable thing happened - all of her senses came rushing back at once.

She opened her eyes. Everything was slightly unclear for a moment. She was lying in a stark garden, where the spindly trees did not give fruit or grow leaves. There were small grey boulders dotted about the rectangular-shaped garden. It had a Japanese feel to it: but instead of stone statues of Buddha, there were grotesque statues of the Bogie Beast. At the far end of the garden she could see a thorny hedge, yet no bird song could be heard anywhere. Rising up high out of the ground was an unnaturally tall rock which resembled a badly carved obelisk. It was as red as blood, and Jesse shuddered at the sticky liquid that she now saw oozing from the pinnacle, trickling down to feed a small red stream.

'Where are we?' she slurred, finding it hard to talk properly. Her tongue still hadn't stopped tingling completely from the effects of the acrid potion, which she could now taste. It was vile.

'We are not sure. It looks like some kind of memorial garden, maybe, a sick joke created by the Beast,' the Dragon Hunter said. 'But we will be out of here and out of this stinking city soon.'

'Tis a fine planning that we be a-making,' Iggywig added, looking pleased with himself. 'A-failing it can not be.'

'I don't like the sound of that,' Jesse said pessimistically, not yet turning her head to see the Iggywig that she would not recognise. 'It sounds too easy.'

'Tis a simple plan, but easy? Iggywig be a-trying not to be a-thinking about how tricky it be.'

Twisting her head, Jesse flinched as though a whip had been cracked. She simply stared for a full thirty seconds at the Iggywig she could not comprehend. Her mouth had dropped, and her eyes were as wide as dinner plates. This was unbelievable! He was so magnificent, so beautiful - as if a caterpillar had transformed into a radiant butterfly. Though he had small, neat wings tucked up on his straight back, he was not a butterfly. He stood fully seven feet tall, slender, and almost human but for his wings and talons. There was a silver glow around his muscular body as if moonlight was shining. From his woven silver hair, handsome elegant face, and kind bright eyes starlight glimmered.

'Iggywig?' Jesse whispered in disbelief.

'Tis a strange creature Jesse be a-seeing,' Iggywig said softly, and his voice sounded like chimes ringing a soothing melody. 'Tis my pretty self you be a-seeing.'

Jesse shot the Dragon Hunter a dark glance. The Dragon Hunter couldn't hold her gaze. He looked away in embarrassment and shame.

'How could you ... kill ... Iggywig?' she snapped. 'How wicked and-'

'Tis a-pleasure to be killed now and again,' Iggywig cut across her. 'Be not too hard on the kind slayer. He be a-doing Iggywig a-favouring.

See?' He flapped his wings furiously and began to rise above the ground. 'Tis a-good fun a-flying.'

Jesse couldn't help a smile. Her old cuddly Iggywig was there somewhere inside, even though the creature before her was a complete stranger.

'I'm sorry,' she said awkwardly to the Dragon Hunter. 'It's just - just that I miss my old Iggywig.' She looked at the Gobbit. 'Will you ever return to your old self?'

'The next time Iggywig be a-dying.'

'But that could be years and years.'

Iggywig nodded, starlight glittering around his face. 'Jesse be a-getting used to the new Iggywig in time, maybe?'

Jesse felt incredibly selfish for running on about how she'd missed the old Iggywig. How must the new Iggywig be feeling? How thoughtless she'd been.

'You really are extraordinarily handsome,' she said.

'Iggywig be a-thanking Jesse.'

A gurgling noise distracted their attention. The red liquid spluttered and spat from the rock.

'What are we going to do to get away from this place?' Jesse asked, sitting up now with plenty of colour in her face. She couldn't take her eyes off the red liquid rolling down the side of the rock and trickling into the stream. She had the horrible feeling that it was blood. Whose blood she dare not consider.

'We be a-having a simple plan,' Iggywig said, and they huddled together and began to whisper.

Jesse moved not one muscle as the elfins marched passed, transfixed by the pulsating towers of light they held in their tiny hands. She and Iggywig and the Dragon Hunter had been sucking *Chameleon Sweets* for ages and were perfectly blended, backs against the wall of a smoked glass building. It towered above them further than they could see. They were waiting for the right moment to move off again, but there were many creatures walking up and down the main streets. And there were even more patrolling the skies on dragons and griffins and horned flying beasts which Jesse couldn't name. Every now and again, a blob of black slime would appear on the glistening pavements or roads. From it would emerge a hideous, dripping, oily creature, which would taste the humid air with a black forked tongue, then dissolve again and disappear. And there in the background of her mind she could hear the fiddle music - haunting and hypnotic.

For almost an hour, the monotonous noise of sirens had echoed in their ears. Thick beams of searchlight shone through the smoked glass windows of the thousands of skyscrapers. Inside, Jesse was shocked to spy children working at what looked like computer terminals, and in offices, and behind reception desks. The tower-carrying elfins were never far from them, and Jesse wondered if the children were being controlled or monitored in some way.

'Who are those children?' Jesse asked, as they sneaked along a few more blocks towards the outskirts of the city.

'They are your half brothers and sisters,' the Dragon Hunter said.

'But there are thousands of them,' Jesse said, not hiding the shock in her voice.

'So it seems,' the Dragon Hunter said. 'It's part of the Bogie Beast's plan to control his children's minds.'

Jesse suddenly recalled Brimbalin's words about the Bogie Beast and shuddered.

'Whatever you do, do not listen to your father's music. It holds immense power that will entrance his children's minds.'

Ever since she had arrived Jesse had been fighting with the Bogie Beast's music. It had poured into her mind like a waterfall, its icy, haunting melody trying to control her. Even though she had not been entranced completely, she could see that there were many who had been entranced, and this disturbed her greatly.

'We have to help them,' she blurted out.

'What?'

'Must be the effectings of the Sleep Walking Potion,' Iggywig said. 'Jesse be a-little cuckoo crazy.'

'I'm not crazy.' She swung around to face the Dragon Hunter, and her blending blurred, revealing a shimmering image. 'You should feel for them more than most. After all, they are our half brothers and sisters.'

'Stand still,' the Dragon Hunter hissed, 'and be quiet. You will blow our cover!'

There was another group of tower-carrying elfins approaching them along the street. From the opposite direction, she could see two more groups of elfins headed in their direction.

'I don't care about our cover,' Jesse snapped. 'We have to help them. It's the only chance of rescue they will ever get. No-one, especially our own flesh and blood, should be allowed to suffer like this. Now will you help me or not?'

'Be quiet,' the Dragon Hunter whispered, as the elfins closed to within twenty yards of their position.

'Will you help me?'

Fifteen yards and closing ...

'Jesse, stop talking. You are shimmering. Your blending is breaking up!'

'I don't care-'

Ten yards from them the elfins paused, gazing around, looking at the towers, then back again towards their position.

'Yes. I will help you,' the Dragon Hunter said heavily, his brow furrowed.

Jesse smiled, and froze. An elfin walked quickly to her position, extending the pulsating tower. A strange high-pitched singing squealed in her ears. She began to feel as if she would topple over, dizzy from the excruciating noise. She suddenly felt very drowsy again, and realised in a dreamy kind of way that it was the towers that had sent her into a stupor the first time. The power of them was overwhelming her. She felt her legs begin to buckle.

As she started to slip, the Dragon Hunter lunged out, kicking the elfin aside. The tower crashed to the floor, and from the shattered glass a living force whooshed into the air, narrowly missing the retreating elfin. The force looked like a thin, red and green striped mist. It was a funnel shape which extended about five feet high.

It curled as if smoke into a loop and pelted to within an inch of the Dragon Hunter's face.

'Please help the rest of my people,' the living force croaked. The words came as strong and emotional thoughts, telepathically delivered. 'Free them before their spirits' die forever.'

'Who are you?' Jesse asked, the drowsiness beginning to pass somewhat.

'I am a Vadi, a spirit of the underworld. I and my kind were tricked by the Beast to perform tasks that are not true to our nature.'

It paused and Jesse felt an overwhelming feeling of sadness pouring from the Vadi.

'We hate ourselves for what we have been made to do. But we were powerless ... until now. Thank you for releasing me. You see, it is our force, our power that holds the children here in this city of slime. We were once peaceful creatures, who helped the dead to cross the River Between Life and Death. Now we have become ... something ... evil and dark, trapped for centuries, where our hatred has grown because of our imprisonment. Please free my people. It is the only way to free yourselves and the children. For each Vadi freed, scores of children awake from their stupor. Quickly, before it is too late. Smash the towers!'

There was no time for debate, or further questions. Great columns of black slime were rising from the streets. High above them in the smoky glass buildings, Jesse could see dozens of children banging on the windows, desperate to be freed, now that they were no longer entranced by the imprisoned force of the Vadi.

'Do something!' Jesse yelled, the sight of the children sending a chilling ripple of concern through her. 'Hurry!'

With each tower that was smashed by the lightning speed of the Dragon Hunter, Jesse could see more and more children and more and more Vadi freed. The Vadi rose high above them, joining together to make a massive eddying force that looked like a red and green tornado. The elfins, too, were clearly grateful of release from their tower-carrying task. They ran shouting with joy, dodging passed the dark rising pools of slime. Some elfins knocked towers from the hands of other elfins who were emerging out onto the streets. More Vadi rose, and more elfins ran, until the streets were swarming with creatures.

'Skyward!' they yelled. 'The volcano is closing up. Skyward!'

'You must save yourselves,' the first Vadi to be released urged. 'The volcano will be completely sealed within two minutes! Go! There is little sense in you being captured. You have started the children's escape. We will do what we can to help the rest. Skyward! Fly!'

There seemed little point in arguing with the Vadi. Jesse watched as it zoomed into the air to join with the other Vadi who had escaped. Together they created an enormous swirling force, which looped the loop and hurtled down to the streets, knocking towers from elfins hands and releasing more and more of their kind. This in turn released hundreds of children from their stupors, and they took to the skies on dragons and griffins and other winged beasts.

Suddenly, Jesse found herself thinking about Jake Briggs. It was time for her and her companions to leave, too. She transformed into her dragon self and the Hunter rode on her back, with Iggywig flapping his tiny wings at a fantastic speed. As they soared higher and higher, and closer and closer to freedom, Jesse's mind flitted from Jake to the children, who were still under the mind control of the Bogie Beast, slaves in the glass skyscrapers. It was a terrible decision she had had to make, but the Vadi had been right. There was no point in risking capture.

Besides, it wasn't all doom and gloom. Ahead of them and below, indeed all around, thousands of children and elfins were escaping on winged beasts, pouring through the ever narrowing gap of the volcano's mouth.

As they hurtled through the hole to freedom, Jesse gasped. The landscape beyond the Mountains of Mourn had changed out of all recognition.

'The Rumble,' she muttered. 'Look what it has done!'

Ten

Island Gloom

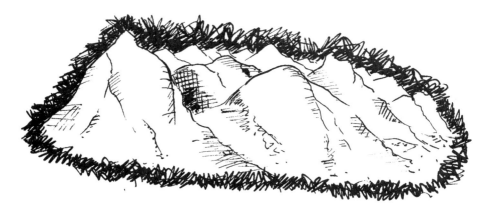

'Amazingly, as the Rumble reached the foot of the Mountains of Mourn, its hunger stopped. Or rather, the force-field that protected the mountains turned the Rumble in upon itself, so that it headed back the way it had come.'

'It's a miracle,' Jesse said, agog. They were standing at the foot of the Mountains of Mourn, peering at the shining sight all around them.

A rather noble, slender creature had paused, standing on a small boulder. He was dressed in a long purple coat, baggy yellow trousers, and a green and red hooped shirt. His beautiful features glimmered with starlight, tiny golden sparks flashing about his head. His elfish face was pointed and wan, and his green eyes glowed as though on fire. In every other way, he resembled the transformed Iggywig, who had been keen to shake the wizard's hand at length and tell him what a great honour it was to meet him at last in the flesh. Iggywig had informed Jesse that the wizard had mastered the Art of Tongues, and could speak fluently in every language there had ever been, except common witch-slang, which he'd said was too disturbing to utter or think about. The legendary Gobbit had announced himself as Zarlan-Jagr, a white wizard from the Union of Thirteen, to a tumultuous round of applause. He now cleared his throat to continue to speak to the gathered multitude.

'From the safety of these mountains, I could hardly believe my eyes. The landscape was re-appearing from a brief hibernation, a state of non-existence, and with it appeared the people and the buildings. It was rebirth for all things; and people's attitudes were changed, too. I ventured into Alisbad and could not believe how much the folk there had changed. Their discontent became The Calm, and once again there was a spirit of friendship, trust, and tolerance. The Kingdom of Finnigull has been healed. Praise to Boeron.'

'Praise to Boeron!' the crowd echoed.

'What about the mining goblins?' yelled an elf. 'I bet they are still as evil as ever!'

'You would lose your bet,' Zarlan-Jagr said.

'All is calm, all is quiet.'

'And Loath Town? What of that foul place?'

'From all accounts - although I've not been there myself - the darkness has gone. Only good lives there now.'

'And Dendrith's Castle?'

'Hard to believe, I know, but the darkness has gone, except ... well ... I'm sad to say, Dendrith herself has escaped the beneficial effects of the Rumble. It is rumoured that she and her dark followers have headed for the Island Gloom, the only land to escape the influence of the Rumble in the Kingdom of Finnigull.'

Jesse felt her chest tighten. Dendrith could be extracting the Glow right now. They had to hurry before it was too late.

'How did the Island Gloom manage to remain untouched by the Rumble?' the Dragon Hunter asked, watching Jesse transform into her dragon self and take to the sky.

'The sea around the island had a similar effect to that of the force-field around the Mountains of Mourn. The Rumble has a weakness, it seems, which it cannot penetrate. It hit the shore and rebounded back on itself.'

'Ooooh!' roared some of the crowd. 'Wow!'

The multitude muttered excitedly amongst themselves.

'Now, let us not talk of what has been, but

what will be, my friends,' Zarlan-Jagr said. He hovered slowly into the air. 'Come and join all the city folk of Alisbad in a party of great rejoicing. You are all invited. It begins tomorrow, and lasts for the next forty days. Food and drink aplenty is free!'

The crowd cheered, and many of them took to the skies on their flying beasts, heading with Zarlan-Jagr for Alisbad. Jesse and her companions flew north-east towards the dark blot of Island Gloom. Jesse prayed they were not too late.

Jesse landed on the mirky beach, carefully stepping over the washed up litter and rubbish which festooned the Island Gloom. Ahead, she could see rusty skeletons of ship wrecks and oil-slicked sands as they sneaked cautiously along the beach towards the old pirate stockade.

'The stockade is like no other pirate stockade that I know,' the Dragon Hunter whispered, as they rested behind a large rock just a hundred yards from it. 'Its stakes are made from sharpened crystal. Each one is as thick as a man's body and twice as tall. Legend says it was built by giant troll pirates thousands of years ago.'

'How do we get inside?' Jesse wanted to know.

'One of the stakes is really a secret entrance,

but more than that, I don't know.'

'So we fly over?'

'Tis a fine idea Jesse be a-having,' Iggywig said, 'but not a-possible one.'

'Why?'

'Come,' the Dragon Hunter said, leading the way across the sand. 'We will show you.'

They paused behind the last rock - big enough to hide them just fifteen yards from the stockade. The stakes hummed and buzzed deeply, as though an electric current was running through them. Jesse watched as Iggywig picked up a hand-sized pebble and threw it high over the crystal stakes. There was a loud crack, a flash of blue light, and the pebble shattered into thousands of tiny fragments.

'Tis a-forcing field of much power,' Iggywig observed.

'So what now?' Jesse asked shakily.

'We need to find the stake that's the secret door,' the Dragon Hunter said.

'How?'

'I don't know,' the Dragon Hunter admitted. 'But every minute we spend talking is another minute wasted.'

'Yes, you're right,' Jesse agreed. 'Let's go to the stockade and search for the door.'

Even as they pelted across the sand to the first of hundreds of stakes, Jesse felt a little deflated. It seemed an impossible task, an impossible race against time. But they had to try. They had no choice.

'What should we do?' Jesse asked.

'Do not touch the stakes,' the Dragon Hunter warned, nodding to a skeleton slumped on the sand to their left. 'You do not want to end up like him.'

Jesse shuddered at the thought, and tried to refocus her mind on a possible solution. But something was bothering her. There just wasn't enough time to check every stake.

'We have to split up,' she said. 'We can check more stakes that way.'

'Agreed,' the Dragon Hunter said. 'You go left. Iggywig go right.'

'And you?'

'I'll run around to the other side and make my way back to you, Jesse.'

Jesse nodded and began examining the stakes as closely as she dared. She didn't care for the humming sound coming from them. But what to look for? Symbols? Writing? Glyphs? Something to reveal the secret door must be visible, she reasoned. But she was not convinced. It seemed too easy, to have a symbol or sign, or secret password. And there was something else that seemed too easy, she thought.

'We got to the stockade too easily,' she

muttered aloud. 'Something is wrong. It feels terribly wrong - like a trap or ...'

'Well done, my pretty,' a familiar voice hissed behind her. 'How clever you are.'

Jesse jumped and swivelled around, kicking sand as she span.

The witch was leaning against a rock, watching, picking her lunch from her teeth with a long talon fingernail. She was grinning strangely, a grin that almost resembled a snarl.

'Jagdrith?'

Jagdrith grimaced, glaring madly at Jesse.

'Like a fly to a web,' Jagdrith laughed. 'How satisfying. You'll be as dead as my aunt -

Gwendrith - by the time I've finished with you. Revenge will be bliss.'

Jesse fumbled in her pocket for a *Chameleon Sweet*. Now would be a good time to blend. Instead, she felt the flexible rubber of the Homingball which Iggywig had given her.

'What are you doing?' Jagdrith asked, clicking her fingers and producing a wand from thin air. 'What are you up to?'

'N-n-nothing,' Jesse stammered, her mind racing for something to say to stall the young witch. 'I'm just getting the key to the door.'

'What?' Jagdrith said, confusion in her voice.

'Yes,' Jesse lied. 'I have the key to-'

'There is no key!' Jagdrith shouted, sparks flying from the tip of the wand. 'You are up to something. Take your hand out of your pocket slowly and drop whatever it is you are holding onto the sand.'

Jesse eased her hand out of her pocket.

'Drop it!' Jagdrith demanded. 'Or I'll kill you where you stand!'

In one swift movement, Jesse threw the Homingball at the witch, diving head first onto the sand and covering her head with her hands. The Homingball hit the witch straight between her eyes, and exploded like a grenade. But instead of pieces of shrapnel, thousands of thorny tendrils lassoed around Jagdrith's head and body and legs, wrapping around and around until all that could be seen was her screaming mouth.

As Jagdrith tried to move towards Jesse she hit the sand with a dull thud, writhing and rolling, desperate to escape her bonds.

'I'll get you for this, Jameson,' she threatened. 'This is not over yet!'

Jesse twisted onto her side and sat up, ignoring Jagdrith's threats. She was watching in amazement, as the Homingball remade itself out of nowhere. It was spinning in a figure of eight so fast that it looked like a blur. With a snap of completion, the ball reappeared and plopped onto the sand in front of Jesse.

She bent down and picked it up. As she began to slide it back into her pocket, she had an idea. Maybe she could use the Homingball to her advantage. But she would have to make some distance between herself and the screaming Jagdrith. The young witch's whining voice was getting on her nerves.

A minute later she was far enough away from the witch to begin her idea with a clear head. She stepped back twenty paces, tossing the Homingball in her hand. She took careful aim, and hurled the ball at a stake with all her might.

Jesse had expected the ball to hit the stake and explode, somehow revealing the hidden door. It was a weak idea, but she was desperate to try anything. Her deep desire to rescue Jake had spurred her on. She fought hard to block the thought of Jake having his Glow extracted. She had to get inside the stockade - she just had to.

Then it happened. Instead of exploding and remaking itself, the Homingball passed clean through the stake. It was the door! It was also much too easy, Jesse thought, as she ran at the stake herself. She closed her eyes as she pushed out her arms in front of her to cushion the impact. But there was no impact. Just like the Homingball, she glided through the stake with only the slightest resistance - a kind of light tugging all over her body, as if snared by a prickly hedge.

She was in! And what she saw all around her did not please her.

She was standing at the end of a very long courtyard. About three quarters of the way up the red walls she spied grotesque gargoyles - at least a dozen or more dotted around. Towering crystal stakes pulsed primary colours, rising like giant vampire teeth. They cast long dark shadows through the mirky grey haze that hung over the large flag stones.

Her heart beating wildly, Jesse listened to the distant roar of the sea, and much closer the buzz of the stakes. Could Dendrith be waiting behind one, ready to pounce? And where was Jake? Perhaps it was too late?

She saw the Homingball spinning along the stones towards her. It stopped at her feet and she bent down, picking it up. Cautiously she sneaked forward between the stakes. Her footsteps slapped the hard floor, echoing around the courtyard walls. She glanced up at the stone gargoyles, their twisted gruesome features glaring back. Then one pair of the stone eyes glowed green, blinked, and turned to stone once more. Jesse's stomach heaved.

As she walked passed the final stake, a small arched doorway ahead leading into another courtyard, Jesse saw the huddled figure of Jake Briggs. He was curled up, rocking back and forth, against the far wall.

'Jake!' Jesse cried, and pelted through the arch and into the second courtyard. 'Are you all right?'

It was only when she'd reached him, wrenched his tear-sodden hands from his face, and saw the horrified look in his red raw eyes that she glanced back.

Kildrith stepped into view through the arch, his wide-brimmed black hat barely shading the maze of scars on his face. Behind him, shaking her fist threateningly, strode Jagdrith. Then, in glided Dendrith, her long black hair billowing out in its own icy breeze. Her bulging eyes were insane pits of darkness. She cackled madly, and clapped her hands with hysterical delight.

'Jesse, my little pretty,' she drooled. She wafted her bony hand about like a mad conductor without an orchestra. Jesse felt a blood-chilling blast of frozen putrid air stinging her eyes. 'What a lovely surprise. I'm so glad that you could join our little party. I believe you already know my two colleagues?'

Kildrith and Jagdrith hissed and spat like rabid animals.

Jesse ignored them, and tried to get Jake to his feet. 'Come on, Jake,' she whispered. 'I'm taking you home.'

'Isn't she sweet?' Dendrith said sarcastically. 'She really believes that she can escape with her entranced friend. So rare - an innocent gull.'

'What d'you mean entranced?' Jesse asked, trying to lift Jake up.

Jagdrith laughed coldly. 'She really is clueless, isn't she?'

'As I told you, sweetie slug,' Dendrith said, brushing a lock of blonde hair from Jagdrith's face. 'Just like her father. Not an ounce of intelligence between them.'

Dendrith began to laugh madly again, and her companions joined in, howling like banshees.

Dendrith narrowed her eyes, and real malice descended upon them. 'What do you think you are going to do with that ball you keep tossing, sweetie? Bowl us over like pins?'

Again they howled at the witch's wise crack. Their madness echoed around the courtyard like a thousand of their twisted kind.

Jesse said nothing. Her mind was stuck in first gear. What should she do? Where was the Dragon Hunter or Iggywig? She needed them. She scanned the top of the courtyard walls for signs of help, or escape. She saw none.

'Let us talk,' Dendrith said seriously. 'There are debts to be paid, Jesse Jameson. You owe me more than blood or that precious Golden Glow of yours. You murdered my sister, and for that you will die a slow and painful death.'

'Your sister was trying to kill us,' Jesse said, feeling anger rise in her throat. 'We were defending ourselves. If you were in our position you'd have done the same.'

'Defence or attack? It matters not. You killed Gwendrith, and she is lost now; destined to wander that foul place between life and death - never at rest, never at peace. And for that you are to blame!'

Jesse saw a glimmer of real sadness in the witch's wicked eyes. She had been hurt badly by Gwendrith's death. But she didn't feel sorry for her.

'You escaped me twice before,' the witch went on. 'But not this time. Third time lucky ...

three is my lucky number … and today is your unlucky day.'

They all laughed, and began to glide effortlessly across the flag stones towards Jesse. Ten yards from her, they split up. Kildrith went to the left of Jesse, and Jagdrith to the right. Dendrith hovered directly in front, her fingers twitching sparks of dark magic from the tips. All around her, from darkness which clung to her cloak, her Surgeons began to appear, twisting razor-sharp scalpels in their many tentacles.

'Make the extraction as painful as possible!' Dendrith ordered. 'But do not damage her Golden Glow! It is mine! At last! Mine forever!'

Kildrith was the first to attack though. He slipped his hand inside his vaporising chest, slid it out dripping a green phosphorous substance, and tossed a small metal box onto the flag stones. He uttered mystical words never heard by human ears. The shining box flew off ahead of him, humming like a bee, rotating at a tremendous speed towards Jesse.

Jesse ducked, knocking Jake to the flag stones. The box hit the wall behind them and exploded with a loud bang. Dust and brick and mortar showered them. Jesse saw blood on her hands as she took them from her ears. She felt her scalp. It was sticky, warm, and bleeding badly.

'Come on, Jake,' she said, trying to haul him

to his feet. She had noticed in the far corner of the courtyard, a manhole cover. Maybe, just maybe, they could get to it, lift it open, and descend into ... what she didn't know. But it was a chance of escape. Better than waiting for death to come. 'Come on, Jake! We have to run!'

'Don't make me look into your eyes,' Jake said strangely, keeping his head bent low.

'What?' Jesse sounded completely confused.

'My eyes are not to be looked into.'

'We haven't got time for this now. Come on.'

'I don't know how,' Jake went on. 'But the Bogie Beast has cursed me.'

'Up!' Jesse yelled, raising him to wobbly feet with all her strength. 'Come on!'

'Don't look, please. I don't want to hurt you.'

Jesse stared at Jake blankly. 'What?'

He shrugged, and tilted his head.

Jesse screamed at the sight of what lay buried inside Jake's eyes, just a split second before the Dragon Hunter strode through the far arch, swinging his sword of light from side to side.

'Blachgarglach!' Dendrith yelled, and with a wave of her hand the stone gargoyles came to life. They leapt down onto the ground.

The Dragon Hunter cut clean through two of the gargoyles with a single sideways blow. Their magical flesh instantly turned from stone to dust, as they shattered on the flag stones. Three more keeled over with his second blow, but he was outnumbered. Three quicker gargoyles jumped onto his back and strove to wrestle him to the ground. He swung around with tremendous speed and one flew off, smashing into the wall. The other two scratched and clawed and plunged sharp teeth into his armour, desperately trying to rip it off like a seagull ripping a shell from a crab.

Iggywig appeared from nowhere, spitting a *Chameleon Sweet* into his hand. He raced across to the Dragon Hunter, and yanked a gargoyle from his back. It shattered into dust as it hit the ground. The Dragon Hunter dispatched the remaining gargoyles with ease, and together with Iggywig by his side, he strode towards the two witches and warlock.

The Surgeons were closing in on Jesse. She was slumped against a stunned-looking Jake, a bundle of limp arms and legs. Her eyelids fluttered like butterfly wings. She was losing consciousness.

'Sister!' Dendrith wailed. 'We need your help, my dearest sister! Come now! Come from that place between light and dark! In the name of all that is evil and foul - help us defeat our enemies! The time has come for vengeance! Your killers are here. Come now, sister!'

The manhole cover flipped open. It twirled round and round and round until at last it rested in peace on the flag stones. What looked like ghostly gnarled fingers slowly slithered out of the black hole, preceded by the misty shadow of a beast that was tall and thin and unspeakably ugly. It was the moaning phantom of Gwendrith.

Jesse's world faded in and out of view. There were three rolling images - the courtyard battle, Jake's mad eyes, and the unnerving vision of the Bogie Beast. She tried to focus on getting Jake to his feet, but her own legs wouldn't move.

Something black and slimy was rising out of the flag stone floor. No, not the flag stone floor, but out of Jake Briggs's ruined eye sockets. It was the Bogie Beast. His essence was pouring out like black tar.

'Revenge is ours, sister,' Dendrith cackled. 'Kill them all!'

Gwendrith was gliding towards Jesse. She heard her awful moaning, and felt the icy chill of her spectre. With a mind full of confused images, Jesse began to crawl across the stones. She had to get away. But she would not leave alone. She was taking Jake with her. She grabbed his hand and began to pull him across the rough floor.

Running at full pelt, the Dragon Hunter raised his sword of light. Dendrith had her back turned on him, urging her ghoulish sister on. One blow would be enough to kill the witch.

Bang!

The Dragon Hunter hit the invisible force field around Dendrith with a mighty crunch. He rebounded backwards, and smacked the ground hard. Blood trickled from his mouth. His body was motionless.

Jesse had managed to crawl across the courtyard to the corner where the manhole was gaping dark and gloomy. Her head was pounding intensely, but at least the revolving images had ceased. She glanced over her shoulder, but couldn't see the Bogie Beast. Had she imagined his evil presence?

'Be a good time for the getting away!' she heard Iggywig shout. 'Run, Jesse Jameson. Take your chancings!'

Jesse peered into the hole, and could see the faint glimmer of a wall ladder, leading down into a pit of blackness. 'Follow me,' she ordered Jake, who was also moving more freely now.

Before she disappeared into the mirk, she glanced across the courtyard. Her heart lurched at the sight of the Dragon Hunter motionless on the ground. She started to climb back out of the hole.

'GO!' Iggywig yelled. 'BE A-SAVING YOURSELF AND YOUR FRIEND!'

Kildrith and Jagdrith were gliding quickly towards her. Their faces were full of fury. Their eyes were glaring insanely.

Iggywig clicked his fingers twice, and the stream of sparks issued from his fingertips knocked Kildrith against the wall. He smashed his bulk against the brick, and slithered unconscious to the ground.

Jesse descended into the darkness, the chilled and salty air wrapping around her like a damp, cold cloak.

At the same time that Iggywig sent another vicious charm towards Jagdrith, Dendrith conjured magic of equal power. The spinning disc of red light cracked Iggywig on his temple, and he crumpled to the floor, groaning and clutching his bleeding head. The light from the ruptured disc poured into his ears and mouth until his mind was full of the ranting menace of thousands of insane taunts and spells. He dug his fingers into his scalp, desperate to release the racket, but the bedlam wouldn't stop.

A moment later, Jagdrith screamed and held her eyes. Iggywig's Blinding Charm had done its work, despite his own ensuing madness. Thick brown mucus had completely covered the young witch's eyes, and she was hissing in agony.

'I can't see!' she yelled, panic in her thin reed-like voice. 'Help me! I can't see!'

'Help yourself, you pathetic wreck,' Dendrith sniped. 'Use your dark magic. The children are getting away!'

'But I can't see?' Jagdrith sobbed. She

sounded as if her heart was breaking.

'Do you need to see to avenge your Aunt Gwendrith's death?'

'But I don't know what to do?'

'How familiar that little excuse is becoming. First you let Jameson win the Shape-Shifting Challenge. And now your lack of imagination to create a counter-charm disgusts me. You soil the reputation of a thousand generations of witches. You are useless.'

'But I don't know how to counter the charm? It is too strong.'

'Then stay blind and sobbing forever!' Dendrith growled, gliding quickly towards Jesse's escape route, her Surgeons in tow. 'You are no daughter of mine if you cannot help yourself with all the dark magic you have inherited from me. You are an embarrassment to the great line of Driths. Enjoy your weakness, my child. While I enjoy the hunt and death of our enemies!'

'Oh, mummy, help me, please!' Jagdrith blubbered.

'Don't call me mummy,' Dendrith snapped.

'But ... mum- I mean, mother, I need your help.'

The witch ignored her daughter's whining, blanking her as if she no longer existed. A dark cloud of disappointment trailed out behind her.

Gwendrith was already in the sewer, giving

chase to her quarry, as Dendrith jumped into the blackness of the hole to join her.

Eleven

Stepping Stones to Freedom

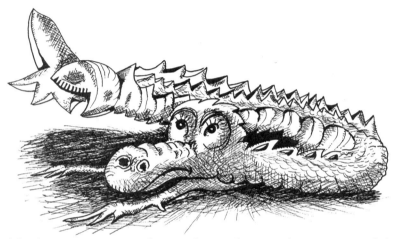

Twice Jesse thought that they would be captured by the pursuing witches. But twice the dark tunnels forked and allowed them time to gain a few precious minutes. It's like a maze down here, Jesse thought. We could be going round in circles. Luck has been with us, but for how much longer?

It was hard to see far ahead in the darkness of the sewer. Although Jesse wasn't convinced that this was a sewer. To her mind it looked too dry and clean, much more like a series of secret smugglers' tunnels.

After a few minutes progress, her

observations were proved right as they hurtled around a bend, arms stretched out to deflect any unseen obstacle. They had stumbled upon a hoard of pirates' treasure in a small cavern. It was dimly lit by a thin shaft of light that shone down through a hole in the roof. There were caskets of rum, and chests of glittering gold and silver, jewels and trinkets of every kind.

Jake hurried to it, pawing it gleefully.

'Leave it,' Jesse said. 'We have no time for this. The witches are gaining on us.'

'But we're rich,' Jake cried. His voice echoed around the cavern spookily. 'Just look at it, Jesse!'

'Keep your voice down,' Jesse hissed.

Jake began to fill his pockets with gold coins.

'Put them back!' Jesse demanded. 'They will slow us down. And you'll be able to hear the clinking a mile away.'

'Sod the clinking,' Jake said, ramming a few more into his already bulging pockets. 'They'll make me rich beyond belief.'

'I'd rather be poor and alive, than dead and rich for a minute.'

'Chill out, Jesse,' Jake retorted. 'If you don't want them, then that's fine. But I'm taking as many as I can carry. So keep your nose out of my business.'

Jesse knew it was pointless to argue. Even

in the dim light of the cavern, she could see a greedy glow in Jake's eyes. The look she saw there frightened her. She still hadn't shaken off the vision of her father's black slime pouring out of Jake's eye sockets. She doubted if she ever would. It had seemed so real. She allowed a dark nightmarish thought to rise in her mind, and tried hard to subdue it, but it was too strong: her father's essence was inside Jake. Somehow, the Bogie Beast had escaped the Mountains of Mourn, and was now hiding inside Jake, waiting for the right moment to reveal himself through her best friend. Jake Briggs was host to the darkest force of evil any kingdom had ever known.

'What are you staring at?' Jake snapped. His brow was furrowed, and he somehow looked a lot older in the shadowy light.

'N-nothing,' Jesse stammered.

Jake grinned strangely.

'Are you sure?' he said.

Jesse stared at him, unable to look away.

'It's you, isn't it?' Jesse said, beginning to tremble from head to toe.

'Yes,' Jake said levelly. 'I've waited such a long time to be this close to you. We can talk now, as father and daughter. Together we will make a formidable partnership.'

Jesse glanced over her shoulder. The cursing witches were getting closer.

'Don't fret about them,' Jake said. 'When the time comes, I will crush them like ants beneath my boot.'

'I have nothing to say to you,' Jesse said, gritting her teeth.

'Oh, please, don't let us rake over old ground, Jesse. The past is gone, never to be undone. But the future, our future will be glorious.'

'I don't think so,' Jesse said, and she turned her back on him to walk along another dark tunnel.

'Wait,' Jake said, and Jesse thought she heard a note of desperation in his voice.

Jesse continued to move away, feeling empowered.

'Please, don't go. You're all I have left now. I can never return to my city beneath the Mountains of Mourn. There is nothing left for me there anymore. The children have all gone, and with them-'

'Your power,' Dendrith cut across him.

Jesse swivelled around to see the witch standing at one of the entrances to the cavern. Her hair and cloak billowed out behind her. The stench from her ruinous body filled Jesse's nostrils, and she gagged.

'Country air!' Dendrith laughed. 'Isn't it grand?'

'You are sick,' Jesse managed, swallowing

down bile.

'Thank you, child. You have such an elegant way with words.' She narrowed her eyes towards Jake. 'As does your father. What was it you were saying about losing all of your power?'

Jake slumped to his knees, groaning. His face darkened, and from his eyes poured the black slime of the Bogie Beast. As it hit the rock floor it rose up into a towering figure of dripping black goo. It shot a flaming blast of dark liquid from its mouth.

Dendrith waved her hand and the liquid splattered across her invisible force field like vomit splattering a glass window.

'I may be weakened,' the Bogie Beast snarled, 'but you are no match for me, witch. Leave while you still can, and take that ghoul with you.'

Gwendrith's ghost howled shrilly at her sister's side. Tendrils of ectoplasm reached out towards Jesse's face. The Bogie Beast snapped out a slimy pointed arm, slicing the tendril in two. Gwendrith cried in pain, retracting the ectoplasm back into her formless body.

Dendrith hissed, spat, and leapt forward, arms and hands spread like eagle's talons. Her hair was standing up on end like a peacock unravelling its feathers. Her black eyes were demented with rage.

The Bogie Beast laughed and strode

forwards to meet the witch. As they locked in mortal combat, snarling and gnashing, biting and gouging, spitting and hissing at each other like wild predators, Jesse seized her chance. She raced across to Jake and hauled him to his feet. With one arm clinging around her shoulders for support, she manoeuvred him out of the cavern and along a narrow tunnel.

They heard the cries of pain echoing behind them, and Jesse prayed that their battle would be long and hard and mortal for them both.

Five minutes later, the tunnel ended abruptly. They skidded to a halt, pebbles and dust tumbled over the edge of a gaping pit. Above them, the tunnel ceiling had become lower, so that they were now crouching on their hands and knees. Below them a bleak abyss dropped steeply. Jesse squinted against the dimly lit wall on the opposite side. It was a long way across the abyss, and on the far side she could just make out a gigantic figure of eight symbol which had been carved into the rock. The very low ceiling continued all the way across to the other side.

Then, Mystic Mo's prophetic words came somersaulting into her mind:

Beware of the abyss with its hidden stones.
Step on them in a figure of eight,
Otherwise you'll perish by the force of your own weight.

Reveal the steps you must take,
By tossing sand like fishing bait.

'We're finished,' Jake said gloomily. 'Unless you can fly.'

'I could,' Jesse said. 'I could transform into a dragon, or any creature I want. But I can't think of a creature that would be small enough to make it across such a confined space, and strong enough to carry you on my back.'

Jake let out a deep belly laugh. 'Still got a sense of humour, I see. Excellent. Fly across?'

'But I can,' Jesse said. She now realised that Jake had been under the influence of the Bogie Beast on the several occasions she'd been a dragon in his company.

'P-p-prove it,' Jake scoffed. He held his sides, still laughing hard.

'We haven't got time for this. There has to be another way. Let me think ...'

'You crack me up, Jesse Jameson,' Jake said, slapping her on the back. He unclipped his useless mobile phone from his belt. He'd tried it a few times, but he guessed that the battery was damaged. No signal at all. He held it out to Jesse. 'Why don't you call a taxi?'

'Stop it,' Jesse scolded. 'I'm trying to think. We haven't much time.'

Hysterical, Jake clipped the phone back onto his belt. 'We're as good as dead,' he said, through howls of laughter. 'We might as well jump, and get it over and done with.'

Jesse thought about Mystic Mo's words again. She glanced down at her feet, and saw that the floor was covered in sand.

'Fishing bait,' she murmured.

Jake held his sides and kicked his legs, consumed with laughter. Everything sounded funny to him now. He was delirious with fear.

'My dad used to toss handfuls of maggots into the water when he wanted to lure fish. That's it. Yes!'

Jake was out of control, squirming around like a helpless maggot. He pounded his fist on the floor in an effort to stop laughing.

Jesse grabbed a handful of sand and tossed it into the abyss. Some of it fell out of sight, but many grains landed on small rocks. No, not rocks!

'The stepping stones! Just as Mystic Mo predicted!' Jesse yelled gleefully. She scattered more handfuls of sand as wide as she could. More round stones appeared. There were hundreds of them. 'Hurry, Jake. Follow me.'

'You're joking, right?'

His own laughter had stopped abruptly. Jesse's words had been like a sobering slap.

'Tip out the coins, and fill your pockets with sand.'

'What?' Jake felt his bulging pockets, and

pulled out a few coins, examining them. 'Where did I get these from?'

'I'll tell you later. Just do as I say. The sand might just save your life.'

Jake did as he was told, emptying gold coins onto the ground, and refilling his pockets with sand.

'Look,' Jesse said, pointing halfway across the abyss. A deep cold darkness surrounded each stone. 'That's as far as I can throw the sand. We don't know where the stepping stones lead after that. The more sand we have, the better our chances.'

'But how do you know which stones to step on?'

'The figure of eight, over there on the wall. That's the clue that Mystic Mo told me about. It all makes sense.'

'To you, but not to me. Who's Mystic Mo?'

'Not now, Jake.' She looked squarely in his eyes. 'You have to trust me. All right?'

Jake smiled. 'All right. So what next?'

'Take off your socks.'

'What the-'

'Just do as I say,' Jesse said, taking off her own socks. 'Fill them with coins, and tie them at the ends.'

Jake did as he was told, and then put his shoes back on.

'This is weird. What are we doing with the

socks of coins?' Jake said.

'This,' said Jesse, and she tossed a heavy sock onto the stepping stone which was the closest to her. It landed with a jangly thump. It skidded a little on the grains of sand and then stopped.

'It's safe,' Jesse said. 'I'll go first, just in case the stone crumbles or descends into the pit or something.'

'I know,' Jake said sarcastically. 'You'll turn into a butterfly and save yourself.'

'Something like that,' Jesse said, and she leapt across the black pit onto the first stepping stone. Carefully, she bent down and blew the grains of sand away. The stepping stone she was standing on vanished.

'What are you doing?' Jake said.

'Why make it easy for anyone who's following us?'

'Good thinking,' Jake said. 'But from now on, I'll blow the sand away. Once you leave that stone, I have no way of knowing where to step. Some sand, please.'

'Sorry,' Jesse said, and sprinkled a little sand back onto the stone.

'Thanks.'

'Anything for a friend.' She picked up the sock and threw onto the next stone. 'Safe.'

She stepped onto the stone, and glanced across at the pattern of the figure of eight. There were three choices before her. Each stone was side by side. Which stone? She tossed the sock onto the furthest to the right. For a moment, it seemed safe, but then it started to crumble ... and the stone and sock of coins fell swiftly out of sight into the dark pit. They fell a long way before they hit the bottom with a tiny splash.

'Be careful,' Jake said in a trembling voice.

She nodded, and concentrated as she threw her last sock onto the middle stone. She waited a full minute before she was convinced that it was safe. Her heart hammered in her chest, as she stepped gingerly onto the stone. It was safe. She sighed with relief.

The next three stones were also safe, and now Jake was just one stepping stone behind her. All the stones behind him had vanished.

'All that sand blowing has made me feel giddy,' Jake confessed. 'And I think I'm afraid of heights. I feel terribly sick every time I look down. Hurry, please.'

'I'm going as fast as I can,' Jesse said, throwing another sock onto a stone. 'Try not to look down.'

At last they reached the middle, and Jesse scattered sand ahead of her. There seemed to be more stones than ever, all crammed together like blunt teeth rising out of the darkness.

'This is ridiculous,' Jake said, sounding fed up. 'Which way now?'

'Be quiet, I'm thinking.' Jesse stared at the figure of eight, and glanced back at the way they had come. 'Damn,' she mumbled under her breath.'

'What's wrong?'

'Nothing,' Jesse lied. She wished she could see all of the stones behind her. It was the only way she could visualise the curve of the figure of eight. Straight ahead or curving left?

She tossed her last sock onto the stone directly ahead. The sock and the stone disappeared immediately, crumbling into the darkness.

'Pass me your socks,' she said, taking them carefully from Jake. 'Thanks. I'll try not to breathe in too often.'

Jake smiled. 'Prime mature cheddar,' he joked.

She lobbed a sock onto the left hand stone. Two minutes passed before she plucked up enough courage to step onto it. The next five steps seemed easy to locate, and now they were just six stones from the other side.

Behind them, not that far away, someone screamed agonisingly. There followed a victory roar, and a moment of silence. Muffled, echoing movement could now be heard getting closer and closer. The victor was pursuing them.

'Hurry,' Jake urged.

The next sock hit the stones and burst open,

scattering coins into the abyss.

'Is it safe?' Jake asked.

'I'm not sure,' Jesse said. 'I don't think there's enough weight on it to test it.'

'What should we do?'

The commotion behind them was growing. Someone was hurrying through the tunnels at great speed.

Jesse kissed Jake's last sock and winked at him. 'Here goes,' she said, and threw it onto the stone. It slid like an ice skate on the coins and rested just an inch from the edge. It teetered back and forth, back ... and ... forth ... then stopped.

A minute went by. The sock held steady. And so too did the stone. Jesse jumped. Jake winced. She landed with a thud, snatching the sock as it tumbled over the edge.

'It's safe,' she yelled, kissing the rescued sock again. 'Five to go.'

'Sick,' Jake groaned.

Stone four was safe, too. But there were a multitude of stones before them now. It was impossible to work out which were the safe ones.

Jesse chucked the sock onto the stone slightly to her left. It felt the right thing to do. The sock hit the stone and burst ... coins rained down into the abyss.

'No!' Jake yelled.

'It's not over yet,' Jesse said calmly.

'Don't talk rubbish,' Jake said. 'What chance do we have now? One wrong step and we are dead.'

'If I transform into a baby dragon, then I'll be heavy enough to test the stones, and nimble enough to fly to safety if I get it wrong. Either way, we find out which are the safe stones.'

'You're mad,' Jake said, shaking his head.

'Try not to scream, Jake,' Jesse said.

'What the?'

Jesse transformed into a small green dragon in a few seconds, and hovered just inches from Jake's blood-drained face. He was trembling uncontrollably, eyes wide and bulging, lost for words. He would have screamed but his throat was dry and constricted with shock.

'Sit, before you fall over,' Jesse said, through her dragon mouth.

Jake slumped down obediently on the stone.

Jesse tested each stone until a clear pathway could be seen to the other side. She transformed back into herself, and helped the shaking Jake across the remaining stepping stones. She put a comforting arm around his shoulders and together they walked into another maze of tunnels.

The welcome light at the end of the tunnel came half an hour later. Jesse clambered after Jake through a narrow gap that emerged into a blaze of brilliant sunshine. They were standing on a beach of white sand. Rising high above and behind them they could see huge chalk cliffs and caves. The cliffs looked as if they would crumble at any moment they were so weak and weather-beaten. However, they formed a formidable barrier arching around them on both sides, so that they were trapped by them and the foaming sea ahead.

'Now what?' Jake said weakly.

Jesse scanned the cliff tops and saw three figures. They were waving, and shouting, although their voices were carried on the wind and were lost. As Dendrith staggered from the cave entrance, clearly injured, blood dripping from her face, one of the figures dived over the edge of the cliff … transforming into a huge boulder.

The witch hissed and waved her hand and a disc of red light span like a Frisbee at Jesse's head. She ducked, rugby-tackling Jake to the sand. The disc exploded above their heads. The noise made their ears ring.

Jesse looked up to the cliff top and thought she recognised the Dragon Hunter and Iggywig silhouetted against the skyline.

'So who's that?' she gasped, glancing at the speeding boulder.

Jake barely had time to gather his thoughts, let alone answer.

The boulder crashed onto the swaying body of Dendrith. The witch let out a hideous shriek of agony. Black acrid smoke poured out from beneath the boulder. All that remained visible of the witch was a tatter of her black cloak. There was a moment of silence, and then as the boulder transformed, the ghost of the dead witch whooshed up into the air, howling and cursing like a Spriggan.

From the cave Dendrith was joined by her howling sister, and together they attacked the transformed wizard, Zarlan-Jagr. But their ghostly spectres were no match for the legendary Zarlan. He swatted them away like flies with the back of his hand, as he strode across the sand to Jesse and Jake. He uttered an animal grunt, and the two ghosts vanished.

'I'm sorry I was a little late,' he said softly, bowing long and low. 'But it took me a while to reverse the Madness Charm Dendrith had cast on Iggywig. Awakening the Dragon Hunter was a little less fraught with danger. I merely tossed a bucket of cold water on his head.'

Jesse laughed and gazed admiringly at Zarlan-Jagr. She was mesmerised by his exquisite features, which glimmered with starlight - tiny golden sparks of energy flashing about his head. His wan elfish face came to a pronounced point at his chin and his green eyes glowed as though a burning forest fire.

'I will escort you all to the Banqueting Hall in Alisbad,' he said, wriggling the fingers of his left ringless hand. His right hand was covered in rings of silver, and upon his narrow wrist he wore scores of jangling bracelets. 'If, that is, you wish to join the celebrations of this great and wonderful new day; the day our kingdom was remade by the Rumble? It would be an honour for the city folk, for they hold you, as you know, in high regard.'

'I would love to visit Alisbad again,' Jesse said. She glanced up at the two figures on the cliff tops. 'But first I have to see if my friends are all right.'

Jesse transformed into a golden eagle and flew up to the cliff top. The Dragon Hunter and Iggywig looked exhausted, sitting down heavily on the cliff top. Jesse transformed into herself and sat in between them. She hugged them for a long time.

'I'm so glad you're both all right,' she said at last. She reached out and gently wiped away a trickle of blood from the Dragon Hunter's lip. Suddenly her mind was elsewhere. 'So when do we leave?'

'Where to?' the Dragon Hunter asked.

'We have to find Perigold.'

'We have Perigold already,' Zarlan-Jagr said. He was hovering beside them, with Jake cradled in his arms. He put Jake down and landed next to them.

'Who's we?' Jesse asked.

'The Union of Thirteen, a small but dedicated band of white wizards sworn to fight for justice and peace. Sadly, we arrived a few minutes too late to be of any real help to Perigold. He was ambushed by Dendrith outside the Knoll of Knowing. A messy business.'

'Is ... he ...?'

Jesse couldn't bring herself to say the word.

'Dead?' the wizard said.

'Yes.'

'He lives-'

'Thank goodness for that,' Jesse sighed. 'When can we see him?'

'Soon. But there is a problem.'

'What kind of a problem?' the Dragon Hunter asked, narrowing his golden eyes, scanning the wizard intently.

'We can not wake him.'

'What do you mean?' Jesse's mind was whirling. 'Is he in a coma?'

The wizard shrugged.

'Injured?' Jesse quivered.

'Not physically. But inside his mind? There is a chance that it is so. We have tried all the magic we know. In this kingdom and that of Troth. Even the magical knowledge gleaned from the human world has had no effect.'

'Where is he now?' Jesse asked anxiously.

'In a safe place, under the protection of the Union of Thirteen.'

'And where is that exactly?' the Dragon Hunter persisted.

Zarlan-Jagr looked around, scanned the beach. 'I can't tell you, but I can take you there.'

'When?' Jesse asked.

The wizard wriggled the ringless fingers of his left hand. A Spiral Gate opened just a few feet away.

'How did you do that?' Jesse said, impressed.

The wizard did not answer. They all followed him into the swirling energy. They set their Spiral Gate Controllers to the colour blue: the Unknown Kingdoms beckoned.

Jesse Jameson

and the Bogie Beast

Glossary

Assassin - a hired killer.

Beastbots - part beast and part robot, where steel, titanium, and micro-chip have been merged with flesh and bone.

The Calm - a term used by fairy people to discuss the general feeling of a place, person, or kingdom.

Emancipator - someone who frees others.

Fairy Time - one day in Fairy Time traditionally equals a year and a day in human time. (see Time Stopper).

Fairy Vision - the ability of fairy people to be able to see into the fairy worlds while in the human world.

Glyph - a picture or symbol representing words or a syllable.

Gravitunnel - a network of tunnels used by Gobbits and others that date thousands of years before Spiral Gate technology.

Gull - a fool, or one easily duped.

Heckles - a large five-sided gold coin that could be exchanged for fifty-three Shindishes. (see Shindish).

Light-lock - used by Iggywig to seal the Gravitunnel and other tunnels' exit/entrance from uninvited users.

Malgrim - One bite of the malgrim and its juices begin a horrible slow-death that poisons the brain. Madness quickly follows an uncontrollable urge to bite every dog or cat in sight.

Rapier - a light slender sword used for thrusting.

The Rumble - partly people's thoughts and actions, and partly a living force, a creature of sorts that feeds from discontent.

Savacat - a wild cat-like scavenger, whose scratch causes a mad fever.

Shapoes - a nickname for shape-shifters.

Shindish - a triangular silver coin.

Stockade - a line of upright stakes used as a defence, and sometimes built in a circle around another building.

Sylph - an elemental spirit of air.

Time Stopper - a magical potion created by forward-thinking Elders so that the same amount of time passed in all the kingdoms, including the human one. (see Fairy Time).

Vadi - spirits that guide the dead to the afterlife.

Warlock - a male sorcerer or wizard who performs the Dark Arts of Sorcery and Wizardry.

One

The Hiding Place

The High Witch, Zundrith, clung to the shadows of the twilight, muttering spells and casting curses into the towering waterfall. As each splash of freezing water fell, it instantly turned into another jagged tooth of ice. The riverbed was a mountainous mass of sparkling teeth that stretched high into the clouds, formed over centuries, ever increasing, and never melting. Though she wished more than anything to move - just one step - she was welded to the river bank. However, she knew who had tricked her, who had enslaved her for almost a thousand years, and it would not be long before she would be free, and then there would be mayhem and carnage and oceans of blood.

'One day soon, my pathetic little retinue,' Zundrith hissed. 'I shall climb this mountain of ice and teeth and blood and bones. I shall conquer this blasted summit, and free you all. Then we will crush our enemies and all who stand in our way. But not before I have my revenge for the sisters held in that damn glass egg!'

In the palm of her open hand, a tiny red flame flickered. She whispered to the flame fondly, in a language so harsh and fetid that to ears other than the darkest of witches its tones hurt like fists punching and pounding. She curled her upper lip into a grimace of pleasure, and sucked the heat from the flame. She watched through squinting black eyes as the thin ribbon of blue smoke snaked into the icy air. She hissed and it turned into a corkscrew of rhino horn, and then exploded into a million tiny fragments of dust. Crushed - as her enemies would be - she studied the gently drifting particles.

Her contorted skeleton-thin body shuddered, and she howled demonically, calling others from the icy wastelands of the Monsterous Mountains. Many thousands of many millions came swiftly and obediently. Dark things floated in and out of focus, huddled around the dirty pleats of her long black cloak, basking in the unnatural nightfall that surrounded her.

'Go, my pretties,' Zundrith whispered coldly. 'Go now and bring the child, Jesse, to me.'

For the latest Jesse Jameson updates visit

www.seanwright.co.uk

Contact the author on

sean@seanwright.co.uk

and let him know what you think about

Jesse Jameson and the Bogie Beast.

THE JOURNEY NEVER ENDS ...